**REDGATE ACADEMY
of Performing Arts**

Adèle Geras was born in Jerusalem. Her early childhood was spent in many countries, including North Borneo and the Gambia. She studied French and Spanish at St Hilda's College, Oxford, and has been a singer, an actress and a teacher of French. Adèle Geras has had more than seventy books published for children of all ages since 1976, as well as a poetry collection for adults. She is a voracious reader and loves the movies, the theatre, knitting, cats, good food and talking. She is also addicted to libraries, and visits her local branch on an almost daily basis.

Adèle Geras lives in Manchester and is married with two daughters.

REDGATE ACADEMY
of Performing Arts

Adèle Geras

Piccadilly Press • London

for Linda Newbery

Printed and bound by Creative Print and Design (Wales),
Ebbw Vale
for the publishers Piccadilly Press Ltd.,
5 Castle Road, London NW1 8PR

Set in Gill Sans, 10.75 pt

A catalogue record for this book is available
from the British Library

ISBNs: 1 85340 559 0 (trade paperback)

3 5 7 9 10 8 6 4 2

Text and cover design by Judith Robertson

"OK, you guys, listen up!" Nish leaned against the table and looked around at the crowds of assorted hopefuls draped over benches and propped against walls and sitting on the few chairs ranged round the walls of the Ballet Studio. Sparko looked at him: crewcut hair and a sweatshirt with a couple of alphabet letters on the front so closely intertwined that no one even tried to read them. A baseball cap completed the outfit.

Nish's real name was Warren Nash, and Nish was short for 'initials'. Nish loved monograms with a passion. Almost any would do, although he'd probably have drawn the line at BSE. Posh designer initials were best of all, and he was saving up for trainers emblazoned with his top faves of all time: DKNY. Nish was OK, for someone in Year Twelve, but he liked to pretend that he was American. All this *listen up* nonsense. He'd probably been exposed at an early age to the TV show "Fame" and had modelled himself ever since on that teacher . . . the one who said all the stuff like: Fame costs, and here's where you start paying. In sweat.

Sparko liked Nish. One day, when Sparko was first at Redgate, Nish had watched him in the ballet studio, and he had been able to tell that Sparko was still self-conscious about being a boy and at the same time a good dancer and had made a point of coming up to speak to him.

"You're good, kid," he'd said. "Don't let anyone put you off. They'll try, don't worry."

"They already do," Sparko answered. "My dad and my brothers think I'm about to drape ostrich feathers round my neck and stand in for Lily Savage. Or worse, even."

Nish grinned. "Tell me about it! You can thank your lucky stars, though, that at least you're not black. I get all that plus the 'natural rhythm' routine on top of everything. No one said it was going to be easy, right?"

"Right!" Sparko agreed, but he'd felt better at once.

Now Sparko smiled at Nish, who looked as though he was just about to say something along the lines of *I'm talking sizzle*, which was the best line in the whole of the "Fame" series. In fact, what he said was: "This year, I reckon we ought to do something different. I've had *Nutcrackers*, pantomimes, Nativities and so on up to here." He flourished a slim hand elaborately across his forehead. "Can anyone think of something original? We've only got a few weeks to put the whole show together, and we need ideas fast."

Duh, really? thought Sparko. Nobody ever needed ideas slowly. He decided to retreat into his own thoughts until the whole thing had been thrashed out by the eager beavers (Matt the Dweeb, Carrots, etc.), who always wanted to have a say in things. He'd join in all right, at the proper time, when everything was worked out and all he had to do was something simple like audition. For the moment, while the preliminaries were going on, he glanced around the room for Coral. Where was she? Sparko searched out Julian Philips, the school hunk, and there he was, posed on the piano stool, behind Nish but somehow very visible, with his little crowd of followers elegantly arranged around him. But no Coral. Where was she? True, ever since primary school she had been about as punctual as a hibernating hedgehog, but still, surely she wouldn't miss a chance to be a mover and a shaker? To direct the way things were going?

Just as he was thinking this, right on cue the swing doors

to the studio whooshed open and she – what? breezed in? sashayed in? swung in? glided in? A bit of all of those. Sparko smiled to himself. Coral could never just *come in*. An entrance: that was what this was, and she made sure that every eye in the room was on her as she pushed through to the front. Someone else would have sidled in at the back and stayed there, but not Coral.

"Sorry, Nish," she said in that voice . . . the one that carried from one end of the room to the other without ever seeming actually loud. How did she do it? Another of the mysteries surrounding Coral and something to do with acoustics and voice production and boring stuff like that, but actually just part of the magic. Sparko felt his heart jump about in his chest. He was used to this. It happened whenever he saw her, and it was no different now from that first time: in the corridor outside Mrs Fletcher's class, all those years ago when they'd both been five years old.

"What are you called?" she'd said to him then.

"Simon Parks," he'd answered, "but my mum calls me Sparky."

"I like that name!" she'd smiled at him, her eyes shining, and she'd put out a soft brown hand and stroked his hair. Sparko remembered even now, after nearly ten years, the feeling of pure happiness that had flooded through him then. He'd loved her ever since, and anyone who said little kids didn't know what love was was talking pure drivel and had forgotten what it was like to be young.

Things had changed since the Mrs Fletcher days, not least their names. Coral used to be Carol.

"But that's ordinary, don't you think, Sparky?" she'd said three years ago, when they were about to audition for the Redgate Academy of Performing Arts. "Boring little blondes with pink lipstick are called Carol."

"If you say so," Sparky muttered. He didn't know much about lipstick in those days, and certainly not which sort of girl wore what colour, or why such things mattered. "What're you going to be called, then?"

"I haven't decided. Possibly Desirée. Or Melinda. Or Briony." She fixed him with her dark eyes and frowned. "Come to think of it, Sparky sounds a bit babyish for you. You should call yourself something else."

"I like Sparky. It's neat. S. Parks. Geddit? Simon Parks. My real name. And there's the record . . . 'Sparky's Magic Piano'."

When he was four, his mother had found him playing songs (with both hands, almost properly) on the lounge bar upright. She decided on the spot that his musical talent *was* a sort of magic and never stopped telling everyone how brilliant he was. It was embarrassing, but in his heart of hearts Sparky loved being the centre of attention.

"I know!" said the person who was soon going to cease being a Carol for ever. "We'll call you Sparko. That's like your real name, but sort of harder. You want to be hard, don't you?"

Sparko nodded. He'd been trying to be hard for years and years. Just his luck: to be born into a family of cavemen. Apart from his mum, of course. She was fine, and had made sure little Simon (as she called him) had lessons and encouraged him to play the piano whenever there was no one in the bar. The Blue Anchor was the name of his mum's and dad's public house. It was the brewery's really, but his mum and dad did all the work running it, so Sparky thought of it as theirs. His dad was a grown-up caveman, and his two brothers (Nick and Pete, one two years older than he was and one two years younger) were trainee cavemen, shaping up really well for Junior Neanderthal of the Year awards.

Sparky's announcement that he was auditioning for a place at Redgate had produced a contest at every meal to see who could make the wittiest rude remark along the lines of: *Sparky's going to be a pansy/fairy/poofter and learn how to be a dancer.* There were comments about dying swans and wearing tights and lifting hefty ballerinas every day for weeks and weeks. The idea was to make Sparky lose his temper, and if possible start a proper fight with flying crockery involved. That didn't work, because Sparky was ready for them, and whenever they spoke he pretended that they were ducks quacking, or turkeys gobbling, and this tactic enabled him to ignore them almost completely. It drove them mad, and they would stomp off to school in a foul mood while Sparky helped himself to another bowl of cereal. Mealtimes had been hard for years, which was only to be expected when you were a vegetarian in a household of men who didn't consider food had passed their lips unless it was still practically galloping across the plate, preferably dripping blood. There had been jokes about green stuff ever since he could remember, and these were supplemented by the dancing ones, but they didn't work. Sparky had developed a calm exterior over years of green jokes. When they saw that greens and dancing didn't work, they started picking on his "musical talent". Dad, as usual, started it all, this time by cunningly changing tack a little.

"It's a waste," he announced. "Lad's got a talent for music. Play any instrument or compose any kind of tune, he could. If he put his mind to it. But no, he's got to go tiptoeing off to Redgate Academy. What's he going to do for an education, eh? How does he think he's going to get his GCSEs? that's what I'd like to know. Satin ballet shoes aren't going to butter any parsnips. Not when it comes to getting a job in the real world."

"Calm down, dear," Mum had said mildly. "They do academic work at Redgate. I've explained it to you. They just concentrate on the performing arts alongside, sort of."

Snorts all round from Dad and Nick and Pete. Mum continued: "And he may not get in. There's a lot of competition for the places, you know."

But they *were* accepted, and now Sparko and not Carol,

but Coral were just starting Year Ten. Simply by changing the vowels round in her name, his beloved had become an exotic creature. She explained it to him patiently, when he didn't understand it to begin with.

"Coral, silly. It makes you think of turquoise seas and lovely white sand and stuff like that. Brazilian things to go with my Brazilian name: de Barros. My dad might have been useless at sticking around to see his little girl grow up, but he gave me an ace name for neon lights: Coral de Barros. I love it!"

One of the good things about Redgate was the no-uniform rule, and from the first day, "Dress to Impress" had been Coral's motto. She'd never wear a neutral colour where a vibrant one was available, and red was her trademark. She had red skirts, tops, trousers, sweatshirts, headbands and leotards. She had red shoes and red handbags, and her long, black hair and pale golden skin against all that colour made everyone stare at her wherever she went.

"And that, darling Sparko, is the whole idea!" she told him, when he mentioned it once. "I *want* to be stared at wherever I go."

Sparko came back to the present moment and tuned in briefly to what Nish was saying: ". . . so we'll hold auditions this weekend. Starting ten o'clock on Saturday. And are we agreed? We're going to ditch the usual Christmas stuff and go for something more multicultural and abstract . . . possibly something set in the world of homelessness and poverty. A fable for our times, kind of thing. Lots of dance and movement, and really heart-stopping music."

That'll teach me to get lost in daydreams about Coral, Sparko thought. The Christmas show is going to be all dark and meaningful. He felt a pang of regret for the glitzy, tinselly, knees-up sort of Christmas show they'd put on last year, when he'd been such a hit as the Christmas cracker, dressed up in red and green with lightning flashes of sequins embroidered on his back. Still, it made sense. They couldn't put on the same thing every year. Even in the gloomiest of shows, they were going to need good male dancers. And I *am* good, Sparko said to himself. That's why it's all worth it – the stupid jokes, the name-calling, the grief he kept getting from his brothers – because I'm good. I can dance. Really dance.

The door at the back of the studio opened again, and this time it was as though a soft breeze had come along and pushed it gently. A blonde head came in first, and the rest of a slim, tall girl followed. Sparko recognised her as the new kid who'd just transferred into Year Ten. She'd appeared at the beginning of term from London. Lydia, that was her name. He hadn't had much chance to talk to her yet, but she seemed painfully shy.

"Sorry," she almost whispered. "I thought it said one o'clock . . ." Her voice drifted away, and Sparko doubted if anyone had heard her, except him, and he only did because he was sitting near the door. She looked so bewildered and

13

lost that he felt immediately sorry for her. She pushed a strand of hair out of her eyes and gazed around for somewhere to sit.

"Here," Sparko said. "Come and sit over here."

Lydia stepped over people's schoolbags and jackets and sat down next to him. "Thanks," she breathed, and Sparko noticed that she was blushing. "Have I missed a lot?"

"I'll tell you later. Nish is just announcing times for auditions."

Sparko looked at Coral to see whether she was burning up from jealousy, because he was sitting next to a pretty blonde girl with delicate wrists, but no, true to form she was batting her eyelashes at Julian. Sparko sighed. Coral never changed.

SUPPERTIME
Sparko

With both parents fully occupied behind the bar, Sparko and his brothers had worked out a timetable which meant that they could mostly avoid one another's company at suppertime. Or rather, Sparko noticed that N1 and N2 (N for Neanderthal) were usually kitting themselves out in Lycra and trainers at about six o'clock for one athletic pursuit or another, which meant that the kitchen would be pleasantly quiet for at least half an hour. An hour if he was lucky. His mum sometimes came in while he was eating to see that he was OK. She worried that vegetarian food wasn't quite the thing for a growing lad, and no amount of statistical reassurance made any difference. Tonight, she put her head around the door just as Sparko was wondering whether a pickled cucumber could legitimately be counted as a green vegetable.

"Nice day at school, love?" she asked him.

"Not bad. I'm doing the music for the Christmas show."

"What about dancing? Aren't you going to dance this year? I was so proud of you last year! We all were."

Sparko snorted through his veggie burger. When he'd swallowed his mouthful he said: "Your nose is getting longer by the second! You were not all proud of me. Our Pete stayed away from rugger practice for ages because he was embarrassed."

"He told me he had a cold!"

"And you believed him? Honestly, Mum, what planet are you on?"

STAND BY!

Auditions for the
Christmas Show
Saturday 16 October 1999
In the Hall at 10.00 a.m.

DO NOT MISS
THIS UNIQUE
CHANCE!!

Lydia hated being new. It was getting a bit better now, but the first few days had been hard, and some people were the opposite of helpful. She'd had the bad luck to bump into Coral de Barros, for instance, right at the start.

"Can I show you where to go?" Coral said, butter definitely not melting in her mouth. "You must be the new girl from London."

"I'm looking for the head's office," Lydia muttered, dazzled by the vision of colour and glamour before her, wondering if all Redgate girls were supposed to look like that and thinking that she would never manage it, not in a million years.

Coral laughed. "Catherine the Great . . . that's what we call her. Her room is along there, and then turn left. You can't miss it."

So Lydia had set off in that direction, and the corridor went on and on for ages with nothing remotely like a head's office anywhere to be seen. Then, when it came to a place where she could turn left, she'd found herself outside the boys' changing-room and they were all coming out and practically knocked her over. She flattened herself against the wall and tried to rise above the wolf whistles and silly noises and catcalls.

"Ignore these uncivilised creatures," someone had said. "They are silly, childish fools who don't know about human behaviour, manners and so forth. I'm Simon Parks, by the way, but you can call me Sparko."

"Thanks," Lydia said. "I was looking for the head's office, but this girl sent me down here . . ."

"Was she wearing a red sweatband?"

Lydia nodded. "I was asking for it, I suppose. Looking lost

and new. You're not supposed to, are you? When you first get to a place."

"Sounds as though you've met my friend Coral. She's OK, really. You have to get to know her."

They were walking along together by this time, and before Lydia could answer and say something scathing along the lines of "I'd rather cuddle up to a boa constrictor" they'd reached the head's office, and Sparko went off, waving happily at her as she stood waiting outside.

Now she was late again. At this rate the auditions would be over before she got there. She broke into a run as she reached the long drive that led from the street to the front steps of the school. The leaves on the trees that lined it were already turning gold and scarlet.

The Redgate Academy, up until about twenty years ago, was the town house of the Redgate family. They were famous for making sweets, like Redgate Rollers and Redgate Roundies, and when they moved to the country they gave shedloads of money to the town and their house was turned into a school for the performing arts. The reception rooms and some of the bedrooms had been turned into classrooms, and what used to be the drawing-room, even though it was called the hall, became a theatre complete with stage lights and curtains. There were still places in the building where you could see that it had once been a posh house: beautiful ceilings and lovely tall windows which must once, Lydia felt sure, have been hung with red velvet curtains.

At least on a Saturday morning, she wouldn't have missed the beginning of any lessons. Ballet was the worst: she was useless at it. Tatty, the ballet teacher (real name Tatiana Borosova, straight from St Petersburg centuries ago via — according to Coral – Loughborough and Milton Keynes), was a dainty old lady with her hair done up in a bun and a lace shawl around her shoulders. She might have looked like Red Riding Hood's granny, but she generally sounded more like the Wolf, especially when she was moaning at Lydia, which she'd done right from the very first day. She'd given up on her. That was how it seemed, anyway. She said much the same thing at every lesson.

"You have perfect ballet body. Is a pity that to go with body you have no sense of the music. A dancer you will never make, but please to try the hardest possible. I accept only maximum work."

But what's the point? Lydia thought every time as she tortured her limbs into the required positions. What's the point of all this when I'm never in a million years going to dance? She thought longingly of her English homework. I never wanted to come here, she thought. Mum wanted me to, that's all. What can I do to convince her that I have no talent at all? That I want a job where looking at me doesn't come into it. I could be a vet. I could go to vet school. I could look after little lambs who'd lost their mother, and feed them out of baby bottles. I could start not caring that my legs wobble and that I can't make my body move properly to the music.

"Coral, on the other hand," Tatty always said, once she'd finished nagging Lydia, "you should be worst dancer of class. You have too much breasts. You have flesh everywhere, but in the bones is the rhythm and this is most excellent."

This made Coral roll her eyes and shake imaginary maracas and wave her hips about and toss her head until everyone was practically hysterical with laughter. She always managed to do this while Tatty was correcting someone's position at the barre or looking more closely at their *port de bras*, the way they held their arms, and poor old Tatty never knew a thing about it.

Lydia admired Coral for her beauty and her glamour, but didn't really like her. Coral had stopped being obviously nasty to her because she knew that Sparko was sort of friendly with her (well, kind and helpful at any rate, and not teasing and horrid). Obviously, Lydia thought, Sparko was madly in love with Coral. And equally obviously, Coral was not in love back. She had her sights set a little higher: on a Year Twelve boy called Julian, who looked like a walking advertisement for something. Deodorant. Lager. A silver car. Coral and Julian were not exactly an item, but they very soon would be if Coral had her way. Julian's girlfriend,

Louise, was on the way out and didn't even realise. Would Sparko spend more time with her, Lydia, if Coral was busy hanging around with Julian the whole time? Probably not.

In the hall, the auditions had started. Carrots was at the door, making sure everyone came in quietly. He was Matt the Dweeb's sidekick, and his red hair meant that most people forgot he was really plain John Davies.

There was Matt himself, sitting at a table with Nish Nash, who was directing the whole show. Poor Matt. When he was sitting down, you could see that he was really quite good-looking, but standing up he was so tall and skinny that very few people could afford, as Sparko put it, the climbing equipment to go up to his great height and investigate what his face was like up there, where the air was thin and only mountain goats could survive. And Dweeb was a terrible name, but what could you do if your real name was Deebles? Some people were unlucky all round.

"Hello," he said to Lydia. "Is your name down on this?"

He waved a sheet of paper with some names on it at her, and she said: "Lydia Stevenson, that's me."

"Right. Singer, dancer?"

"No, not really. I don't know."

Matt frowned and peered at her through a fringe that could have done with trimming. "Acting, then. You look right for Mary."

"Mary?"

22

"You know . . . Jesus' mother."

Lydia blushed. "Well, yes, but you did say it wasn't going to be a proper Nativity play . . ."

"It isn't," Matt said. "We're kind of transposing it to now. I'm going to put together an outline of the story, and when we've got a cast they'll improvise and bring their own perspectives to the thing . . . do you see what I mean?"

Lydia nodded politely and wondered privately what was wrong with buying lots of copies of a play that someone had already taken the trouble to write out in full. Then everyone could just learn their part and rehearse and the whole thing would be much easier.

"Now," Matt went on, "you're a young girl and you're pregnant. Your boyfriend is useless, but you love him anyway. Your baby's due any day. You've been sent to this bed and breakfast, and a real no-hoper of a landlord says at first there's no room. You have to try to convince him."

"You mean," Lydia's heart was thumping so loudly at this point that she could barely get the words out, "you want me to do it now? In front of everyone?"

"That's the idea. It's an audition," Nish said, taking control. "Get up there on stage and I'll do the part of the landlord. It's an improvisation."

From somewhere in the hall, she heard a snort of laughter. Could it be Coral? Lydia climbed up the steps at the side of the stage, and noticed for the first time that

Sparko was sitting at the piano. He waved at her cheerily, but all she could manage in return was a weak smile.

Nish started yelling at her before she was quite ready.

"Bloody feckless, that's what you are! I don't know what right you think you've got to get pregnant when you don't have two pennies to rub together. I don't know . . . never think, your sort. Never realise that there's honest working people needing my rooms. And where would I be, eh? if I gave beds to every homeless nobody who came along?"

Lydia closed her eyes for a second. Go on, she said to herself. It's acting, remember? You're good at it, otherwise they'd never have taken you here at Redgate. Wait for it to happen. Lydia never quite knew how it *did* happen, but whenever she stepped on to the stage a moment came when she was not herself. And now the someone in her skin was cold, and ill, and hungry. Someone in pain. Someone desperate. Words came pouring out of her mouth almost as though she were a ventriloquist's doll. She didn't know which part of her head or her heart they'd come from, but there they were, in her mouth.

"It isn't my fault. You don't know me. You know nothing about me. I hate this. I hate asking for help from someone like you who had a heart once, I expect, but who's let it get all frozen up and hard so that you can't see when someone's bleeding inside. What about my baby? What's he ever done to you? He'll be born in the street if you don't take us in . . .

do you realise that? D'you want them all to say that about you? D'you want me to stand out here and yell and scream so that all your clients in those poky little rooms, that you sting for every miserable penny they've got . . . so that they'll know what a bastard you are? Do you want that? I may look weak, but I promise you I'd do anything for this kid. Anything it takes. I'll lie down in your foyer and bleed all over your poxy carpet, that's what I'll do . . ." Lydia was almost in tears. A red mist had come down in front of her eyes and she saw nothing. Not the hall, nor everyone else standing round waiting for their turn on the stage. In the end she ran out of words, blinked and came to herself again.

Nish staggered backwards and said: "Wowsers!" Lydia assumed this was a compliment.

"Thanks, Lydia," Matt said as she passed the table. "We'll be putting the cast list up on Monday. Three-ish."

"Right," Lydia said, and she left the room as the next person stood up to do her bit.

Just my luck, Lydia thought, to have ballet last thing on Monday. All day she'd been thinking of nothing but the list. Matt would pin it to the notice-board in the reception area . . . he must know already. At lunchtime in the canteen, she'd glanced towards his table, but he was sitting, as he usually was, in a snowdrift of bits of paper and assorted garments and had paid not the slightest attention to anyone at all.

Coral had walked past the table at least a dozen times, obviously hoping for some hint, or even just for Matt to look up and give her a meaningful smile, but he kept his head down and his hair covered his eyes very conveniently.

Now she had Tatty to take her mind off the list. She tried as hard as she could to remember the sequence of steps she was supposed to be dancing.

"*Nyet!*" came a squeak from Tatty. Lydia had the power to bring her out in a severe attack of the Russian language. "*Nyet*, Lydia! You are like scarecrow! You are supposed to be tree. Wave your branches! Bend in breeze. Bend!"

Lydia bent over obediently in an imaginary breeze and tried not to think about how ridiculous most things in ballet were. You were always having to be something pathetic like a swan or a fairy or something wet and drifty, and Lydia hated it. Surely there were other ways to become flexible?

"Is better!" Tatty pronounced, moving on to her next victim. "Is not good, but is better."

After class, Lydia changed as slowly as she knew how. The cloakroom was filled with voices. *You're sure to be in it . . . you were fantastic . . . Coral, of course . . . and there's only one person who could do that . . . I don't know if it's all going to work . . . they're going to have to make the whole thing up from scratch . . . he's ace . . . what about the music? . . . I daren't look at the notice . . . you look for both of us.* Gradually the chatter died down and Lydia found herself alone. She glanced at her

26

watch. Three twenty. Most people would have gone straight to the notice-board from their last class. Most of them would now be pouring out of the enormous double doors and milling about on the steps. It ought to be safe.

She peered down the corridor. There was still quite a crowd clustered round the notice-board. I'll wait, she thought. I don't want anyone to see me searching for my name and being disappointed. She was just turning to go back into the cloakroom when she heard Sparko calling her: "Lydia! Lydia, come here! You must see this . . . come on, Lydia . . . What are you doing hiding out in the cloakroom? Come on, it's fantastic!"

She turned and made her way to where all the others were standing. There seemed to be hundreds of them, and they all stood back and made a sort of passage for her to walk through. Sparko burst out: "I can't wait to tell you. You've got the main part. You're Mary. The young woman? Mother of the baby Jesus? Nativity play? Ring any bells? You've done it! You're Mary. The main part. Isn't that amazing?"

She looked at the typed notice and saw her name. *Lydia Stevenson – Mary*. And someone called Mickey Flannery as Joseph. *Music and choreography by Simon Parks*. Wasn't he going to be dancing? She searched for Coral's name and found it among the dancers, along with several others, and they were all called simply: *Other parts*.

Lydia blinked. She was going to be in the Christmas show. The main part. She felt suddenly both cold all over and filled with an excitement that she had never felt before. She blushed.

"Well done, Lydia," said Sparko. "You were so good yesterday . . . old Dweebsie was practically in tears. We all were." He grinned. "Except possibly Coral. You notice she isn't here?"

"Should she be?" Lydia was a little mystified.

"Her nose is out of joint, that's all. She'll live. She was such a hit in the summer show last year that I think she sort of assumed she'd be a star in everything for ever and ever amen."

"Why aren't you dancing, Sparko?"

"I'll do something, don't worry," said Sparko. "But if I don't organise the music and choreograph the whole thing, it won't get done. Everyone's always ready to perform, but putting the show together . . . that's something else. It's going to be great, right? Rehearsals start tomorrow. See you then. I've got to go and find Coral."

The crowd around the notice-board had gone. Lydia gazed at the white sheet of A4 and suddenly felt so happy that her feet actually started skipping without her even thinking about it. Wait until Mum hears this, she thought. The main part!

SUPPERTIME
Lydia

"Darling, that's fantastic! I'm so proud of you. You see, there was nothing at all to worry about. I've always known that you could do it. And I knew that all it took was the right school and you would positively blossom."

Lydia looked at her mother. She was so pretty, and so well-dressed and elegant, and seemed to have her life so much under control. Apart from her children, Lydia thought. And being a widow. That was a bit of a disaster. Her father had died before she was born, but she hardly ever thought about him. She did think about her twin sister, though. Lily (that would have been her name) died almost before she'd drawn her first breath, and whenever Lydia felt unhappy or worried or dissatisfied about things she thought: I should have been the one who died. *She* would have been so beautiful, so talented, and exactly the kind of person who sailed through her life without even a hint of disturbance or trouble. Whereas she, Lydia, made heavy weather of stuff . . . that was the way her mother always put it: *Why do you have to make such heavy weather of everything, darling?* Well, now she had brought some really sunny news into the house and was rewarded with her mother's radiant smile and the gift of her approval.

"Tell me all about it, sweetheart," her mother was saying, sitting with her mouth almost open, so eager was she for news of Lydia's triumph. Even though her mum wasn't the kind of over-made-up, pushy monster you saw sometimes at public auditions, Lydia knew that she longed for success. Perhaps she was the one who should have been an actress. If I became a vet, Lydia thought, she'd think we'd both failed.

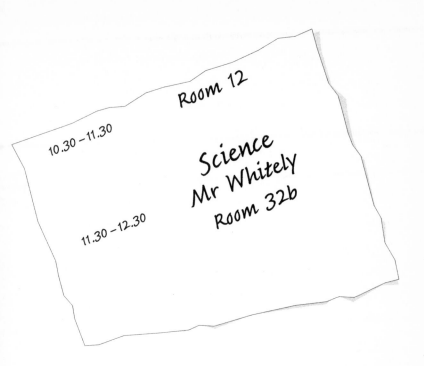

Room 12

10.30 – 11.30

11.30 – 12.30

Science
Mr Whitely
Room 32b

"Now, Miss de Barros, you know why I've sent for you, I'm sure." Catherine Greatorex (aka Catherine the Great, aka Katie G.) stared at Coral from across the scarily empty expanses of her desk. She looked, Coral thought, very imperial in a purple suit with her pepper-and-salt hair up in a French pleat and ready, if her expression was anything to go by, to summon up some kind of schooly-type firing-squad to do their stuff. Coral wondered how *she* ought to look and went in the end for a modified Princess Diana: chin down, looking up through the eyelashes. Innocent. Wronged. This look only worked if you had thick, long eyelashes, and Coral's were practically off the length-and-thickness scale. Catherine the Great was well into her routine by now:

"You know how fierce competition is for places at this school, and therefore we expect the very best from everyone. You are undoubtedly extremely talented, but what you have to realise is that there is more to life than . . ."

Coral tuned out the voice. Teachers, for as long as she had known them, worked off the same script . . . *team spirit, blah blah blah, doing your best, yackety-yak, making the school a pleasant community to live in, rhubarb rhubarb rhubarb* . . . Imagine how much more fun life would be if they were all rescripted by, say, Quentin Tarantino: *You hear what I'm saying, bitch? One more missed essay and you're wasted . . . Your pretty little head'll be all over the blackboard, I hear any more lip from you, you hearin' me?* Or words to that effect.

"Do you understand what I'm saying, dear?" Miss Greatorex was leaning forward, and Coral quickly came out of her daydream. "The academic staff say that you are in serious danger of not being ready for your GCSEs if you continue as you are. Look at this."

She passed Coral an exercise book. Science. That complete scuzzbucket Mr Whitely had shown her exercise book to Katie G. How did he dare? What was she supposed to be looking at? She put on her best puzzled frown and said: "I'm sorry, Miss Greatorex, but I don't know what I'm meant to be looking at."

"Well, it's not the pristine drawings or the thoughtful written work. Try Mr Whitely's comment at the bottom."

Nice one, Coral thought to herself. Quite witty, for a teacher. Quite sharp, old Katie could be, given half a chance. She looked at the miserly little red letters right at the bottom of the page. They read: *Has this been handed in as a joke? See me.* What was she going to say? Her science homework *was* a joke, really, and it was clever of old Whitely to spot it. Sparko would have to be pressed into homework duty for a few weeks until the heat was off, that's all. I have got, she thought to herself, to get out of here as quickly as I possibly can. The head probably still hadn't forgiven her for what had happened at the summer disco. Talk about bearing a grudge! Coral almost smiled as she remembered her own electrifying contribution to the cabaret: an imitation of Katie the Great. She'd put on a smart suit and sung a song called "I wish that I could shimmy like my sister Kate" and done a kind of striptease at the same time. Everyone thought it was hilarious and fell about with laughter, so it was unfortunate that Katie herself should have come into the hall just in time to hear the line that went: "I know she does it, and she does it good." There'd been no point at all in explaining that "it" referred to the shimmy and that the shimmy was just a dance. Some people, especially teachers, had filthy minds and saw sexual innuendos in all sorts of strange places. Nothing better to do with their time: that was Coral's opinion. Now, she smiled her best smile and said in a Princess Diana breathless whisper to go with the tucked-in chin and the upcast eyes: "I really will try, Miss Greatorex. It's just that I spend so much time on the performing side. I really do try at that."

"I know you do, dear," said Katie the Great, quick as a flash, and then she went into the "showbusiness is an unreliable future" routine. Any minute now she'd be quoting Equity figures: 99.999 per cent of all actors, dancers, singers and musicians permanently out of work and enlivening fast-food outlets in every town in the land. M E G A-B O R I N G!

"So I'm relying on you," Miss Greatorex said finally, standing up to show that the interview was over.

"You can, Miss Greatorex," Coral said, rising as elegantly as she knew how from the chair and making her way to the door before another dollop of Teacherspeak occurred to the head. "I promise I'll try to do better. Thank you."

Outside in the corridor, she looked at her watch. Practically lunchtime . . . it was pointless going into a lesson for quarter of an hour, especially as it was Wally Whitely's soppy Science. He deserved nothing but max trouble after that handed-in-as-a-joke routine. She made her way to the cloakroom instead, thinking to try out one of her mum's lipsticks whose name had caught her eye that morning. Crimson Flame was definitely not the kind of colour the deputy head of a primary school should wear. Coral wondered idly whether her own mother went in for

Teacherspeak while she was at work, and decided that maybe she did. How depressing!

The cloakroom was gratifyingly empty. Coral looked at herself in the smeared and spotty mirror and said aloud: "You are the most gorgeous creature in the whole world and Nish Nash needs his head examined. The Christmas show will be drab and uninspired and serve them all right for not choosing you to be something important. You should have been Mary. And Joseph. And all the angels. The whole lot. You could have done it. A one-woman Nativity starring the divine Coral de Barros. Ter-ah!"

She waved her lipstick in the air like a conductor's baton before bringing it to her mouth and outlining her lips. Under her breath, she started to sing "I Feel Pretty" from *West Side Story*. Now that was a proper show. None of this modern, made-up, improvised nonsense. Proper wonderful songs and a real story that made people cry, and above all a show in which she, Coral, had had *such* a part . . . the part of a lifetime. Anita, the second lead, but the one who gets to sing "America". The one who wears the stunning clothes, and sets the stage on fire with her sexiness and pizzazz, a far cry from the niminy-piminy Maria, whose main ambition was for Anita to lower her neckline *one leetle eench*. And there was no point being falsely modest about it: she had caused a sensation. Everyone said so.

"Yes, it was a breakthrough for me," said Coral,

pretending that there was an eager interviewer with his eyes out on stalks sitting in her mirror. She smiled at this invisible creature and went on: "My choreographer, the divine Simon Parks, devised such fabulous dances for me that everyone said . . . all the critics, I mean . . . that the whole emphasis of the piece changed subtly and it became more Anita's story than Maria's . . . do you know what I mean?"

Whenever she felt fed up, Coral relived those three nights last summer when she had glittered and sparkled as never before. And there was something else, which so far she hadn't even said properly to herself. There was a possibility that she could maybe do something more . . . something that would probably never occur to anyone . . . something really different, and out of the league of most of the other Madonna or Spice Girl wannabes who roamed the corridors of this place. During rehearsals for the duet between Maria and Anita, "A Boy Like That", she had suddenly felt a peculiar kind of power rising in her throat as she sang: a sound she wasn't used to coming from her mouth, something she had never heard before. Then someone said (and to this day she had no idea who it was . . . the voice floated out to her on stage from the wings where it was dark): "Coral was absolutely born to play Carmen, wasn't she?"

She'd pushed the words to the back of her mind, but that evening she asked her mother: "Isn't *Carmen* an opera?"

Her mother not only told her all about the gypsy who

made men mad for love but also gave her an ancient tape.

"I listen to it in the car," she told Coral. "It's wonderful. But I didn't think you were into opera. Aren't you planning a career as the next Madonna?"

"I'm not into opera," said Coral. "Just that someone mentioned it the other day, and I wanted to hear it."

"Right," her mother said. "Give it back when you've had a good listen. I'm off to school now."

And off she'd gone, wearing a suit.

"My mum is a teacher," Coral said to the empty kitchen and sighed. It was enough to make a person lose hope.

"I look like my mum," Coral used to moan to Sparko. "D'you think in about a million years I might end up as a deputy head?"

"Never," said Sparko. "They'd never let you within miles of a school. Education may have gone to rack and ruin, but that's ridiculous."

"My mum agrees with you, thank goodness," Coral told him. "That's why she's let me come to Redgate. Sometimes when she gets fed up with all her work, she says she's relying on me to be a big star and keep her in her old age."

But she wouldn't, Coral knew, be best pleased if word of Catherine the Great's little lecture ever reached her ears. If she thought for one moment that Coral was neglecting her academic work, there would be hell to pay. Her mum was supportive and lovely and Coral wouldn't have changed her for the world, but she too tended to come out with those grim Equity statistics at the first sign of trouble. Coral peered into the mirror and wondered why her mood had not improved. If anything, she felt worse now than she had in Katie G.'s office. That was the one part of theatrical life that she found really, really difficult . . . all this being a trouper, and working for the good of the show rather than personal glory.

"We're about to start rehearsing a new show," said Coral now to the imaginary interviewer. "And, of course, one of the things that's most important to me is to be thoroughly professional. A small part is just as important as a large one. A show is a cooperative effort, and everyone is just as vital as everyone else."

She twirled in front of the mirror. The way her skirt rippled round her legs and showed off the red and black striped tights to dazzling effect cheered her up a bit.

To herself she said: What a load of garbage! If you believe that, you'll believe anything. Being a star . . . being better than all the others . . . being the best: that was what it was *truly* about, and anyone who said anything else was lying. Fancy that mousy little Lydia creature whom nobody would look at twice . . . imagine her getting Mary. Maybe Matt or Nish fancied her. Coral wouldn't have put it past them. Boys needed their heads looked at, most of them, and seemed to like all sorts of strange people. Julian's heart was given to

Louise, who in Coral's opinion was nothing but a mousy creature with buck teeth, rather like a very tall rabbit. Not, however, for long. She giggled. Carmen, that's me, she thought. I'm the one, the one who decides who'll fall in love with me and who won't.

The bell rang for dinner, and Coral left the cloakroom and hurried to the canteen, ready to snaffle Sparko and talk to him about possibly helping her with her Science homework for a bit . . . well, for the next year and a half.

SUPPERTIME
Coral

There was such a thing as being too orderly. Her mum was single-handedly responsible for most of the profits of the Post-it company. And she had them colour-coded as well. Something a bit OTT about that, Coral thought, smiling. Pink notes left on the front of the fridge telling her what to microwave that evening. Blue notes left on the table detailing any shopping that needed to be done. Yellow notes with any afterthoughts, deep philosophical insights and general information. Was it any wonder that she never had time to do her homework properly? It was bad enough being a latchkey kid, but being a cook and maid as well was completely out of order. Why did her mum have to be the first in and the last out of her school every single day? Coral knew the answer. It was because she wanted to be a head. Which, she supposed, when she wasn't feeling too hard done by, was exactly like her own driving ambition. Only surely there was something, well, *special* and *different* about wanting to sing and dance? Who could possibly be ambitious to be an even stricter and more bossy kind of teacher? Who'd want to do more paperwork, and come home to tea at nearly six o'clock? Not me, Coral thought. When I'm grown up, this'll just about be the time when I leave home for the theatre.

She pushed dreams of a shiny white car to the back of her mind and wondered about getting stuck into her homework before doing the salad. Suddenly, cutting up tomatoes and slicing cucumbers and mixing a really tasty dressing began to look like a whole lot of fun. She looked through her mother's CDs, neatly stacked on the top shelf of the dresser. It was the title that caught her eye: "Soprano in Red". She'd never heard of the singer . . . someone called Lesley Garrett, but she seemed pretty, and her dress was stunning. I could look like that, Coral thought.

Some of the items listed on the back weren't from operas at all. Coral put the CD in the machine and stood for a long time with the vegetable knife in her hand, lost in the completely strange and unfamiliar music, which seemed to go straight to some place in her head, or her heart, or somewhere, and move her in a way she'd never felt before. The song wasn't sad, but the sound shook her, and her eyes filled with tears, even though she hadn't gone anywhere near the onions.

One of the best things about Redgate Academy was the fact that it was so near the studios of Northside TV. Every sort of place you could think of to eat and drink in had opened in the streets around the school, and Year Teners, who were too young to go into pubs and too poor to eat at the posh restaurants, had chosen Café Lucia as their headquarters. The proprietor, whose name was Ettore, was a skinny version of Pavarotti and would burst into song at the slightest provocation. He would probably, Lydia thought, have preferred it if his café were full of stars from the soaps and afternoon chat-show hosts, but what he was landed with was them: the Redgaters, taking up almost all the space by pushing the tables together. What made Lydia smile was the fact that boys and girls always sat separately. She was grateful that Sparko had taken her under his wing. It was because of that, she knew, that Coral allowed her to sit at the same table as the GQs – the Gossip Queens – who thought they were (and probably were) the only girls in Year Ten worth bothering with.

Lydia stirred her cappuccino and listened. She wondered whether she'd ever be brave enough and accepted enough actually to say something. This was quite a small gathering of the GQs. They'd already had a rehearsal of the show (which didn't have a name yet), and most people had gone straight home after it. Outside, it was already dark, and the windows were streaked with rain. Inside, the steam from the coffee machine and the conversation had turned them foggy and opaque. Coral and Pammy and Shushila were the only ones left at the table. Apart from me, Lydia thought. Pammy was in full flight. She was amazing. No one could call her thin, but she seemed to enjoy her status as an honorary Roseanne figure: sharp-tongued and funny. Lydia wouldn't have put it past Coral to be friends with Pammy because of how slender she looked beside her, but you only had to listen for five minutes to understand why everyone liked her so much. She was easily the most intelligent girl in Year Ten but never gave herself airs because of her cleverness, and generally had a smile on her face. She wanted to be a director.

"Unless," she once said, "someone puts on a live-action version of *Fantasia*, in which case I shall audition for one of the ballet-dancing hippos."

Pammy followed the soaps. She was particularly fond of "Riverview Row", which chronicled the doings of a set of people with more money than sense. Everyone called it "Muesli Mews" after the leading lady's habit of divulging secrets and orchestrating blazing rows in the kitchen before everyone left for their high-powered workplaces. On one occasion there'd been a sizzling snogging session in the area of the breakfast-bar, involving said leading lady and the muscle-bound son of the people next door. This had made tabloid headlines, because he was only seventeen, which was, of course, exactly what the writers of "Muesli Mews" had intended all along.

"Look at this," Pammy said, pushing her copy of *Soap Bubbles* across the table so that the others could see what she was pointing at. "We should tell Katie the Great. She's got strings she can pull at Northside. Isn't she a shareholder in the company or something? They could come down to school and audition us. They're always there quick enough when they need pretty faces to sway in the background for some pop star." She frowned. "No chance for the likes of me, natch. Piers Walden wouldn't have chubby kids . . . nothing but perfect specimens for Perfect Piers." She leaned forward and dropped her voice to a whisper. "Don't look now, but there's a man over there who looks really peculiar. He's staring at us."

"Everyone stares at us," said Coral. "We're worth staring at." She lifted the magazine up in front of her face and peeped around it to examine the man Pammy had mentioned. Lydia followed her gaze. Café Lucia was no more than a titchy little greasy spoon, when all was said and done, and usually there wasn't room for anyone except Redgate kids, and not too many of those, but there he was, taking up the corner table all by himself, skulking. That was the only word for it. He *did* seem to be looking over to their table, but he was also glancing at the boys. He was quite young and quite well-dressed in a smart pair of trousers (French Connection, by the look of them) and a black polo-neck sweater. Lydia had spotted him earlier as she went to get her coffee, but she hadn't said anything.

Sparko, Carrots and the Dweeb were busy discussing the show. They were far too preoccupied to waste time on the young man in the corner. Rehearsals were in full swing now, and it was going to be wall-to-wall Christmas show from now on. Dweebsie had been hard at work on the concept, as he liked to call it. He was explaining it to Sparko.

"The way I see it," he said, "is this. We start in the city, with a kind of jazz ballet of city people – shoppers, policemen, tramps, you know the sort of thing – all milling about, but sharp and witty. A bit like the beginning of *Guys and Dolls*.

45

Know what I mean? Good backing track . . . something cool."

Sparko smiled to himself. Shy, quiet Dweebsie was smitten. He was talking more loudly than he usually did, and there could only be one possible explanation for it: he was trying to impress Lydia. The poor thing hadn't been the same since that audition the other week. Sparko knew that girls regularly discussed who they fancied, how much *exactly* they fancied them, how they compared with someone else that they *quite* fancied, and so on. What's more, they acted on it and didn't just muck about daydreaming. Sometimes they wasted hours on elaborate schemes that involved hanging round the person's house, and at other times they threw any kind of subtlety to the winds and got their best friend to go up to the object of their affections and say: "X fancies you rotten." After that, it was supposed to be up to the boy to do the running. Sparko had had this treatment several times. The trouble was, he was too good-looking. He wasn't being vain: Coral had told him so, years and years ago. It had never occurred to Sparko that he was at all desirable, and as far as he was concerned he'd much rather have been ordinary and faded into the background. There he would be, doing *pliés*, getting on with his life in the back row of the ballet class, when suddenly a girl would loom up over his head and say something like: "Natalie really likes you, you know. She really, really does."

What was he supposed to say? Especially in the middle of *pliés*, with the sweat pouring off him? Usually he just nodded and did nothing about it, and Natalie (or whoever it was that week who'd voted him flavour of the month) faded into the background. But last time it happened, some words actually came out of his mouth before he could do anything to stop them, and before he knew it the gossip was all round the academy.

Sparko's in love with Coral, the whisper went. Coral wasn't best pleased and told him exactly why: "You should never have said such a thing. Never. Even if it's true. People are so silly. You know what they'll think. They'll think that just 'cos you're in love with me, I must be in love with you! It's . . ."

"Embarrassing?" Sparko suggested.

"No." She shook her head.

"What then?"

"I don't know, do I?"

"I do, though," Sparko said.

They were in Coral's house at the time, and he had his foot up on the back of a kitchen chair, with his toes pointed in his trainers, and every so often he bent over from the waist and stretched his upper body all along his leg.

"Stop doing that at once and concentrate!" Coral said. "This is important. Everyone's talking."

"I don't care," said Sparko. "I like it. I like it that everyone thinks we're an item."

Coral squeaked in exasperation. "Well, I don't. And you still haven't told me why I don't."

"You want Julian Philips to think you're available. That's all. I can see what you're doing, even though Louise can't."

"What? What am I doing?"

"You're setting your cap at him. That's what my mum would say. Making a move on him. Something like that."

Now, Sparko looked across Café Lucia to where Coral was sitting. She hadn't denied it. He sighed. It depressed him to see how often life resembled a cheap soap opera: this character loving that one, who wouldn't look at them, and so on, in a kind of Ring-a-Ring-a-Roses. Here was Dweebsie, who, as far as Sparko knew, had never before lowered his head sufficiently even to notice that there were female creatures in the world, struck dumb by the new girl. Who, thought Sparko, if I read the signs right (and goodness knows I've had enough practice at it), is sweet on me. Maybe girls were like ducklings . . . he'd helped Lydia out on her very first day at Redgate, and maybe she'd done that imprinting thing that ducklings did . . . they thought the first creature they saw was their mother. Or something. Life was full of problems, and Sparko tried hard to focus on the show and the music they were going to need for it.

Gusts of whispers and giggles went round the table. "He's getting up . . . he's coming over . . . what'll we say? What'll we do?"

This was Shushila, who was a bit like a butterfly, Lydia thought: pretty and wispy and the very opposite of relaxed. You could practically see wings quivering behind her.

"Right, girls," said Pammy. "Polite and cool. OK?"

"Depends," said Coral. "He's not as bad as I thought. I like his clothes."

"Honestly, girl, get a grip," said Pammy. "He could be a pervert or a kidnapper. Didn't your mum teach you anything?"

Lydia didn't bother to say anything, but watched as the young man got up and paid Ettore. He was so near by now that she could have put out a hand and touched him. He turned round to face them and smiled.

"Hello," he said. "I've seen you all looking at me. Not surprising, really. I've been staring a bit, haven't I? Allow me to introduce myself. Mike Handford, of Northside TV. More particularly, of 'Riverview Row'."

Coral managed not to bat an eyelid, but Shushila fluttered more agitatedly than ever and Pammy's mouth dropped open. The boys, at their table, stopped talking to listen.

"Pull the other one," Pammy said, when she'd recovered.

The young man laughed, and pulled out his wallet. "Here's my card. I don't blame you for not believing me."

Pammy picked it up and examined it.

"I see you're a reader of *Soap Bubbles*," Mike Handford said. "And that's" – he pointed to the article about the search for teenage stepchildren for Piers – "what I wanted to talk to you about."

"How amazing!" said Coral, who had, Lydia noticed, put on a specially deep and seductive voice. "Please sit down."

Lydia stood up, ready to give Mike Handford her chair. But he said: "No, no, that's fine . . . I want to speak to these lads as well." He turned and gestured towards Sparko, Carrots and the Dweeb.

The Dweeb jumped up at once. "Lydia, you can sit here," he said. "I don't mind standing up."

Quick as a flash, Sparko thought admiringly. Not one to let the grass grow under his feet. Dweebsie was seizing the day and no mistake.

When everyone had settled down, Mike Handford began to speak. "You're all from Redgate Academy, I know that. I've been to see your head, and we decided that this was a more natural way to get to know you . . . more lifelike than getting you to do audition pieces in your best voices. We need a girl and a boy to be Piers's stepchildren. Just a couple of days' filming during the Christmas holidays, but of course we need to set it up in advance. You're all great-looking kids, but you" – he pointed at Sparko – "and you" – he nodded at Coral – "seem to be just what's required. Could you possibly come to the studio this Saturday?"

"Oh, how brilliant is that!" Coral exclaimed, forgetting to be impressive and flinging her arms round Pammy's neck. "Of course I can. Can you, Sparko?"

Sparko nodded. A TV soap. Imagine. Something that might even make his Stone Age siblings sit up and take notice.

"Right, then," said Mike Handford. "I'll be in touch with

Miss Greatorex, and I'll see you two on Saturday. Studio six at ten, OK? And call me Mike."

"Yes, thanks," said Sparko, and he stood up to say goodbye in a more dignified position. When Mike had gone, he sat down again.

"Who," said Pammy, expressing what they all felt, "would have thunk it? Ettore, cappuccinos all round!"

BATHTIME
Lydia

Lydia lit two candles that were supposed to smell of lilac but didn't really unless you put your nose practically into the flames. Then she added her favourite dewberry bath oil from the Body Shop to the bath and stepped in. She used to shower quickly in the morning, but in the last few weeks, after reading an article in one of her mother's magazines about the therapeutic value of relaxation in a scented bath before bed, she'd taken to spending the time between finishing her homework and going to bed lying in deep hot water. Turning into a prune, her mother said, but she didn't really mind as long as the radio wasn't on too loud. She used to read, but too many library books had fallen into the water, so now she concentrated on going over things that had happened at school. There was always such a lot to think about.

For instance, tonight there was the problem of Dweebsie.

There wasn't anything wrong with him. He was clever and nice and quite handsome, and it was obvious he liked her. But. But, but, but. What? But what? He wasn't Sparko, that's what. Just saying Sparko's name in her head made her feel quite swoony . . . or maybe the water was too hot? He liked her, but it was clear that Coral was the one he loved. He practically said so all the time. *Perhaps it's his way of keeping girls away from him. Perhaps he thinks they won't pester him or come after him if they know he's already in love with someone else?* Lydia said all these sensible things to herself in her head, but she lived in hope. The magazines were full of stories in which the hero didn't realise until almost the last paragraph that it was the plain, shy girl he'd overlooked all along who was the one for him. Lydia leaned back in the bath and imagined Sparko kissing her. If he ever really did, she'd die of bliss. Shushila was saying something about a post-Hallowe'en disco. Why post-Hallowe'en? Lydia had asked. Because Hallowe'en is over, and we forgot all about organising it, Shushila had answered.

I don't care, Lydia thought. Any disco will be fine. Maybe Sparko will dance with me. I bet the Dweeb is lying in the bath this very minute thinking of me. She giggled. Did boys lie around in baths, dreaming? She found it impossible to imagine.

Coral was walking along as quickly as she could, holding the collar of her coat tightly round her neck against the freezing cold and at the same time trying to explain to Sparko her theory of things being "meant". They were on their way to the Northside TV studio to meet the production team, probably, Coral said, for tests to see whether their faces looked good on camera or something. Mike Handford had been quick off the mark, and the day after the Café Lucia encounter Katie the Great had summoned her and Sparko to the office and gone on and on about their behaviour in public (i.e. at the TV studios) and emphasised that they were not to take anything for granted. The whole production team still had to approve them. And that was only after the audition. Seeing that Coral looked a little startled, she said: "You didn't think you were going to be the only ones they'd be looking at, did you?"

"Oh, no, Miss Greatorex," cooed Coral. "Of course not."

Inwardly, she was seething. That Mike Handford . . . fancy not telling them they would be up against every Tom, Dick and Harriet in town. She tuned in briefly again to what Katie was saying: ". . . and I believe they're having public auditions in London later this month. Of course, you're both at a slight advantage, being locals, I should think."

She went on and on, looking rather severely at Coral. If they *were* successful, they were not to let this media attention go to their heads. It was, she was at pains to remind them, no more than a couple of days' filming at the most, and if she saw that their academic work was suffering (looking at Coral again, wouldn't you know?) then she would withdraw her permission in less time than it takes to say "child star".

"But I see it now – you can see, too, can't you, Sparko? – that the reason why I didn't get one of the main parts in the Christmas show was because this opportunity was just waiting, ready to happen."

Sparko said nothing, just nodded and tried to think of ways to change the subject. He didn't like to point out that all the "Muesli Mews" work would happen long after the

Christmas show was over and forgotten. If Coral felt better about things by thinking they were "meant", then that was fine. He had a much pleasanter life when she was in a good mood, and so did everyone else. She'd even, in the last week, taken to being quite civil to poor old Lydia, which made a change. Obviously she'd decided that Magnanimous Loser and Gallant Trouper was the right image for her . . . so much more flattering than Sourpuss with her nose out of joint!

"Oh, God, Sparko," she said as they approached the Northside studio. "Look at all those people going in . . . they must be the others for the audition. We're here . . . help! Where do we go? You speak . . . I'm terrified."

"Nonsense, Coral. You're never terrified."

"I am, honest. Please, you speak to that person behind the desk."

Sparko went up to the acre of plate glass and silver that was doing duty as a desk. Behind it was a perfect person of the kind seen only behind acres of plate glass and silver: every fingernail sparkling scarlet, and every hair sprayed into place and looking like a metal helmet that even a hurricane wouldn't disturb.

"We've got an appointment with Mike Handford," said Sparko, trying to sound like someone who leaned on acres of plate glass and silver every day of the week.

The perfect person spoke into a state-of-the-art telephone and then turned to him with a slightly more human

56

smile. Evidently the words coming through her earpiece had vouched for them, and now they were part of the charmed circle.

"Mr Handford will be down to fetch you in a moment," she intoned. "Please take a seat over there. Where all the others are. Can you see?"

She pointed to some sofas covered in soft, grey leather. About a dozen others were already sitting nervously on them, but Sparko didn't mind. He sank into the upholstery along with everyone else but Coral stayed on her feet, alert in case any stars passed through the lobby on their way to make a programme. None of the auditionees looked like competition to her. The girls had obviously been reading too many magazines and were dressed in bog-standard Top Shop issue with no sense of individuality at all. Coral was a great believer in individuality. She glanced at the lads only long enough to make sure there was no one there who could be called a catch.

"No one to worry us," she whispered in Sparko's ear. "No lads anywhere near as fanciable as you."

"How would you know?" Sparko said. "You don't fancy me. Or you say you don't. Perhaps you're nurturing a secret passion you haven't told me about."

Coral giggled and carried on awarding marks out of ten to everyone she saw. Then Mike appeared and smiled at them all and said: "OK, this is your first call for the 'Riverview

Row' auditions . . . any takers? OK. Hi, you guys, nice to see you. You ready to strut your stuff?"

"Sure," said Sparko, struggling up from the sofa's embrace. Strut your stuff? he thought to himself. Did anyone still say that? It appeared that Mike was operating from the same "Fame" script as Nish. Sadsville, Arizona.

Studio six turned out to be the biggest room Coral had ever seen in her life. Some chairs were arranged in rows in one corner, and all the hopeful auditionees were told to go and sit down. She couldn't see anything on the studio floor resembling furniture.

"Is this," she asked Mike, "where they film 'Riverview Row'?"

"Gosh, no," said Mike. "Don't you know? I thought everyone knew . . . We've got a whole row of houses back there behind this building, so that everything looks as real as possible. This is just the only studio available now."

A man materialised from the shadows in a corner. Coral blinked. She had never in her life seen anyone half so handsome. Surely there was some mistake, and this was one of the stars? She felt herself grow suddenly out of breath.

"Hello," he said to everyone, but Coral felt as though he was looking only at her when he went on: "I'm Dom. I'd like to thank you all for coming in, and at the weekend as well. We just need to see how you come out on the equipment."

He went over to a camera that was standing in the middle

of the floor like some kind of stumpy, metallic tree and began to call them all out, one by one, in the order in which they were sitting. When it came to Coral's turn, he asked her name.

"Coral de Barros? I'm Dom."

Coral nodded, still dazed. Dom . . . surely that must be short for Dominic? Suddenly, it seemed to her the best, most beautiful name in the world. She must have been mad to think Julian was the best name. It was obviously just a boy's name, whereas Dominic was a proper grown-up man's name. Her heart sank. He was too old for her. He was probably married. He wouldn't look at her. She was a kid, that was all. Coral felt that her heart was breaking even before she'd had a chance of real happiness. In her head, she spoke to the invisible interviewer – the one who was almost always at her side, wherever she went – the same one she'd spoken to in the mirror the other day. It was an in-depth interview . . . *Yes, we were made for one another but it was not to be . . . too old . . . too many people would get hurt . . . I'd never break up his family . . .*

"Just stand over there, dear, and let me get a good look at you . . . very dramatic colouring. De Barros . . . what sort of name is that?"

"It's Brazilian," said Coral, moving into the gaze of the camera. "My father is Brazilian. He lives in Rio. I don't see him very often."

Dom was silent, and Coral just stood there, staring at the bits of him that stuck out from behind the camera. Should she smile? She did, and was rewarded by Dom saying: "Great! Fantastic! Hold it like that for a moment. Great."

She caught sight of herself in the little TV monitor that she suddenly noticed in a corner of the huge space. At first she didn't recognise her own face, but as soon as she grew used to it she had to admit that she looked terrific. She smiled, and said in her head to the invisible interviewer: *My first part was very small really . . . just a couple of scenes in a soap opera, but it did lead on to so much more!*

After Coral had finished, and after the last of the girls – who Coral kept thinking of as "the also-rans", although she would never have admitted it to anyone – Dom turned to Sparko.

"Right, it's the boys' turn now," he said. "What's your name?" She watched Dom telling Sparko where to go and what to do, and saw that he was being just as nice to him as he had been to her. It all meant nothing, all that charm. He was probably lovely to everyone. She sighed. She was being stupid. They were probably not going to be chosen. And even if they were, it was only going to be a couple of days' filming. The idea of her having any kind of relationship with Dom was ridiculous. I might do a lot of pretending and imagining, she said to herself, but I'm not stupid. I'm just a kid to him. Nothing more and nothing less. It would be years and years before she was a grown-up. How depressing was that!

Outside in the street, on the way back to Redgate for rehearsal, Coral said, for about the thousandth time: "How could anyone possibly be better than we are? They couldn't, could they, Sparko? Not better than us?"

Sparko laughed and said in his interviewer's voice (which was what had given Coral the idea of the invisible interviewer in the first place): "Long-time admirers of Miss de Barros have always been unanimous about her great modesty and her longing for invisibility at all costs. *It's not me they're looking at*, she has said more than once. *It's the character. If I can bring that alive* . . . etc., etc., ad infi-blooming-nitum."

They were both late for the run-through.

"Sorry, Nish," said Coral. "It all took much longer than we thought. What have we missed?"

"That's OK," said Nish. "We haven't really started. I don't know why I bother calling for a run-through on a Saturday, but I did want to have a clear couple of hours, which we never seem to get in the week. Anyway, we're all here now, so let's take it from the top. Townies, are you ready for your routine? Sparko? Music . . ."

Sparko had already sat down at the piano. He started to play, and the bodies that had been slumped, slouched and milling about the stage in various stages of relaxation came alive at the sound of his music and went into their steps. They were changed: transformed into policemen, tramps, mothers pushing prams, lovers staring into one another's eyes, and all in the space of a couple of bars. Everyone was transformed and even moved differently from how they normally did. There was Louise, Julian's mousy Louise, suddenly turned into a bent-over old lady, limping, sad. There was Carrots, mild, friendly, jolly old Carrots, quite different from how he always was: changed from one second to another into a thick-set, brutal-looking club bouncer. It really was amazing . . . the way the movements and the music together made everyone into someone else. *It's true what they say, isn't it?* Coral said. (The invisible interviewer was still around.) *It's a kind of magic.* The Inv. Int. bowed his head, stunned by Coral's intelligence and insight. A star in a million, and no mistake! That was what the Inv. Int. thought (invisibly) to himself.

BATHTIME
Coral

Coral felt at home in the bathroom. Of all the rooms in the little semi in which she had lived all her life, she thought this one expressed her personality best. There were plants everywhere: trailing from hanging baskets, on the windowsill, at the edge of the basin. You practically had to hack your way through the undergrowth to get to your toothbrush. The mirror was enormous: Coral had made sure of that, by accompanying her mother to the shop and insisting on it (in the nicest possible way, of course). She peered into it, wondering whether she ought to pluck her eyebrows now or whether she could afford to leave them for another day. Her head was wrapped in a big white towel. She'd put on some new conditioner that promised her totally silky and frizz-free locks, and she was relishing the short time before it was dry to daydream about how her hair would cascade down over her shoulders in an inky waterfall of raven tresses . . . or some such rubbish.

Coral didn't believe advertisements – you'd have to be a fool if you thought a mere product could make the difference between plainness and beauty – but she enjoyed them as a kind of fantasy. The ads were often more fun than the programmes they were slotted into. Still, she said to herself. This is not the time to daydream. There is serious planning to be done. The post-Hallowe'en, no-theme disco was tomorrow night, and she hadn't even made a start on the campaign. That was how she thought of it. She'd wasted weeks waiting for Julian to make the first move, but he hadn't, so it was up to her. She'd consulted Pammy, who was too moral by half. "You wouldn't like it if someone did it to you," she'd said. Who did she think she was? Jiminy Cricket, or something? Coral had said something to the effect that Pammy wasn't her conscience, and Pammy had just laughed. "Conscience? You've got to be kidding . . . you probably don't even know how to spell the word!" Coral and Pammy had been friends for ages, but she could be really, really annoying sometimes. She always thought she was right. She hardly ever misbehaved, either, come to think of it, and if you ever mentioned that to her she said things like "There's no percentage in misbehaving. It's a waste of time."

Coral smiled. Pammy obviously didn't want much from life. Being a bit . . . well, naughty, or bad, or whatever was certainly not a waste of time if it got you what you wanted. And Coral had decided that she wanted Julian. Louise was in Year Twelve, practically grown-up . . . she would get over it. Plenty of fish in the sea, after all. Coral pushed aside a frond of fern that happened to be blocking her view of her left cheek and smiled into the mirror. What to wear? She was going to plan this campaign in the minutest detail.

MISSED HALLOWE'EN?

FORGOT GUY FAWKES?

CHRISTMAS
TOO FAR AWAY?

Don't despair . . . help is at hand
Dance the night away at the

NO-THEME
DISCO

Saturday 13 November
(ooh! spooky . . .)
8 till late

Sparko wondered what his big brother would do for amusement if it weren't for him. He could see, reflected in the mirror in which he was combing his hair, the hideous sight of Nick lying on the bed in his grotty tracksuit, which was an unflattering purplish colour. Nick had been getting at him (what else was new?) and demanding to know where he was off to, all dressed up "like a dog's dinner".

"Better a dog's dinner," Sparko answered, "than a dog's doo-doo."

This had creased Nick up. Then, when Sparko, out of the kindness of his heart, had volunteered some information about the Redgate disco, he'd been seized by such paroxysms of laughter that Sparko feared for Nick's sanity. In the end he simply said: "Calling you pondlife would be insulting to pondlife," and swept out of the room as elegantly as he could. He comforted himself that Nick was jealous . . . he'd never be handsome and debonair! He'd never be able to do *entrechats!* He'd never have the style, the grace, the sheer glamour of the young Fred Astaire . . . well, neither will I, Sparko thought to himself, but at least I come close. He did a pirouette or two in the passage outside the lounge bar just to cheer himself up. His mother popped her head out of the door and smiled at him.

"You look lovely, pet," she said. "Don't be too late now. And be good."

"I'm afraid I haven't got much choice," he said. "No booze, by order of Katie G., and knowing my luck, no girls, either."

"Girls'll be falling over themselves to get their hands on you!" his mum said, unfortunately at exactly the same moment that Nick was coming downstairs. He heard. That was enough.

"Girls wouldn't be any use to him," he smirked. "Try boys. Fighting them away, he'll be. I don't think."

"That supposed to be witty or funny?" Sparko asked, gently, and shook his head.

"Nick, I've told you before!" said their mother. "That's not the way to talk to your brother."

"Leave it, Mum," said Sparko. "I'm off." He waggled his hips and batted his eyelashes provocatively at Nick. "Cinderfella off to the ball."

Standing in the hall, Sparko thought briefly about what Nick had said and how much, a few years ago, such words would have hurt him. Not because there was anything wrong with being gay, but simply because there was nothing more annoying than stupidity and lies, and nothing more frustrating than beating your head against a brick wall. If ever there was a brick wall, this was it. His dad and his brothers had an equation in their heads, hard-wired into them it seemed, which went like this:

Ballet dancer (male) = homosexual.

You could tell them facts until you were blue in the face, to no avail. There were gay dancers, of course, but there were also gay judges, gay doctors, gay publicans, even.

Sparko decided not to let his family spoil his fun and looked around the hall to see who was there. He'd never quite worked out the right time to get to things like this. No one he knew was there yet, except Carrots, who was DJ-ing, and some people he always thought of (unfairly, he knew: they couldn't help it) as the Odds and Sods. Louise. Mickey. Parveen. And there was Lloyd. Though he knew that Dweebsie was around, because he'd seen him sloping off to the cloakroom. Perhaps he was putting on extra-special aftershave, even though he wasn't shaving yet, in a desperate bid to attract Lydia's attention.

While he waited for the really cool types to roll up, Sparko admired the transformation that a few well-placed lights and some well-chosen coloured gels to put in them could achieve. There was even a big glittery ball going round and round and flashing diamonds of light on the walls and ceiling as it turned. Sparko smiled. When he was five, his mum and her friend Sandy had taken him and his brothers to the ballet at Christmas. *The Nutcracker*, it had been, and Sparko still remembered it. Sandy had had to take Nick and Pete home during the interval, because they'd been so bored, but he remained glued to his seat, taking it all in. Even at that age, though he'd been dazzled by the shining lights and beautiful costumes; though he'd believed utterly in the Land of Sweets and the Sugar Plum Fairy; though he'd felt every note of the music in every single cell of his body, he also knew that those were real people up there. They looked like magical beings, but they were flesh and blood, like him. If they could do it, he could too. All the way home, walking along the rainy December pavements, he pointed his toes in his baby shoes as he went and held his arms out to his sides. His mum had asked him if he liked it, and he had no words for her, nothing that would express how he felt. He burst into tears from sheer happiness, and his mum hugged him and said: "Oh, darling, I know! I know exactly. I feel just like that too. Don't cry."

"Will we go again?" Sparko had said. "When will we go again?"

"Whenever we can. I promise."

She'd been as good as her word. Every time a ballet company came to town, they'd be there, in spite of all the noises his dad and brothers had come out with over the years. Now that he knew more about ballet and was actually studying it, he could have told anyone who asked exactly *why* he loved it, and why he had loved it as a child, but no one asked him and so he kept quiet. At Redgate, it was assumed that everyone appreciated the dance, even those who weren't particularly good at it. And if you *were* talented, you got the admiration that in other schools was reserved for the football stars. Sparko leaned against the wall and grinned. That's me, he thought. The David Beckham of Redgate Academy ballet class. He'd been at the school for only a couple of years and already he was one of Tatty's chosen few: the real dancers, as she called them.

"Where is everyone?" asked Dweebsie, waking Sparko out of his daydream.

"Lydia, you mean. I don't know. They're funny, these girls. Spend so long getting ready and prinking in the loo that the disco's over by the time they get here. Never worry . . . that's her, coming in, isn't it?"

"What should I do? Go on, Sparko. Tell us what to do . . ."

"Pathetic, Dweebsie . . . just go up to her and ask her to dance."

"Can't dance. I look a wally. You know that. Why did I bother coming?"

Sparko sighed. "Hopeless, that's what you are. Go and ask if she's hungry or thirsty."

"Then what?"

"Then," Sparko said gently, "take her to get a Coke or a sarnie or something."

"She's probably not hungry."

"You'll never know, will you? until you ask."

"Why don't *you* ask her for me?" Dweebsie took one look at Sparko's face and added: "Oh, OK. I guess she can't bite my head off, can she?"

"That's the spirit. Go for it."

Dweebsie made his way tentatively across the floor. He went up to Lydia, who, to her credit, didn't just turn her back on him but seemed to be listening to the words wafting down from on high. She had her head turned up to look at him. She'd never be Coral in a million years, but that little silver number was stylish in an understated way, and very few girls could manage to look that decent without a bit of lipstick or something. The natural look, that's what Coral called it when someone didn't get all dolled up to the nines, and she always said it with a sort of sneer in her voice, but in Sparko's opinion (and he would never have dared to say so to Coral, for fear of what her reaction would be) lots of boys preferred girls not to be covered in oils and unguents and sticky substances that came off on your clothes. We like skin and hair and lips just as they are . . . that's what he wanted to tell Coral sometimes, when she'd gone a bit berserk with the scarlet lipstick, but he never did. You didn't go hurting the feelings of people you loved to bits. That was obvious.

Well, well, wonders never cease, he thought. They're dancing. Dweebsie and Lydia. Sort of. Jerking about to a rhythm, more like, but still. Lydia looked a bit stunned, but the Dweeb was clearly in his seventh heaven. Where was Coral? Sparko decided to go looking for her. Perhaps she was in the classroom set aside for refreshments.

"I'm going home," Dweebsie said, almost out of breath with excitement.

"But it's early," Sparko objected. "Only just got going really."

What he meant was: Coral hadn't been there long.

Dweebsie was almost stammering. "I know, but the thing

is . . . Lydia has to be home a bit early, and I said I'd take her. Home, I mean."

"You blushing?" Sparko looked at his friend's face, spangled with light from the revolving globe attached to the ceiling. "Hard to tell in this light."

" 'Course not." But Dweebsie was shuffling from foot to foot and Sparko could see he was anxious to get going.

"Had a good time, then? With Lydia?"

This time it was unmistakable. A scarlet flush covered poor Dweebsie's face. He hunted around for some words, and then all he could come up with was: "OK, I s'ppose. Right, I'm off, then."

"See you."

Sparko watched him loping across to where Lydia was standing. As they left the hall, she turned and waved her hand in his direction. He waved back, wondering briefly why it was that he wasn't completely one hundred per cent happy about the Dweebsie-Lydia scenario. Sparko was in the habit of analysing his feelings. Could he possibly be jealous? Rubbish, complete and utter. He had no possible interest in Lydia. But for weeks he'd been a sort of protector for her. His pride was hurt. She didn't seem to need him so much. That was all it was. If he wanted reasons to be unhappy, there were plenty of others, most of them to do with one Coral de Barros. Catastrophe on two long legs, she was. She had managed to turn this whole evening into a total disaster.

She'd arrived fashionably late and looking like a million dollars. He knew because that was the first thing she said to him.

"Hi, babes, don't I look like a million dollars?"

"If you say so. Don't call me babes."

"Sorry, babesie! I do say so. I double say so. I look fan-bloody-tastic, and you deny it if you dare!"

The trouble was, she did. She'd decided that tonight, just for a change, black was to be the colour. Sparko was interested in special effects, so he noticed the way the whole thing was put together: a tiny little short, short dress which looked, on Coral's luscious body, like a coat of high-gloss paint but was probably some kind of nylon or PVC; high-heeled shoes, made out of a few straps woven together into a kind of cat's cradle; and, best of all, a glimmering of gold flakes all over her shoulders and even her face. She glittered. She shone. Her mouth in dark lipstick was like a flower. Sparko found himself almost unable to breathe.

"Can't take their eyes off me, can they?" she whispered in his ear. She meant the Year Twelve boys, like Nish and that tailor's dummy Julian with whom she was so taken. "Come on, you're dancing with me."

"What if I don't want to?"

"Don't you want to? You do, don't you?"

And he did. More than anything. That was what he was here for. That was why he had braved Nick's rudeness and

74

made a special effort with his hair, and (yes, yes, he'd laughed at poor Dweebsie, and he was just as bad) borrowed his dad's aftershave. Being next to Coral made his heart beat faster. Stepping out on to the dance floor with her, he felt like a giant. Part of it was Coral, but mixed into it somewhere was the thrill of being about to dance. About to do the thing he did best. About to be looked at. Envied. He held Coral's hand, and they let the music run through them. They were a part of it, along with the lights and the dazzle and the drumbeat under the tune. We're almost like one person, Sparko thought. It's hard to know where my body ends and hers begins. On and on they went, turning and weaving and shaking, and one by one all the other couples on the floor stood still to look at them. When the music stopped, everyone clapped, and Coral leaned towards him and hugged him.

"Thanks, darling Sparko. That's done the trick. I know it has. It'll all be OK now."

He hadn't known at the time what Coral meant, but he did now. As he made his way home in the early hours of the morning, he was alone. All by himself. The night was still and cold, and the stars looked so close that you could almost touch them. Curls of vapour came out of his mouth and hung in the air every time he breathed out. He'd hardly danced at all after his session with Coral. Mainly, he'd watched, and his reward was seeing a kind of drama unfold.

First, there was Julian and Coral dancing. Julian wasn't a patch on Sparko, but he was OK. Perhaps, Sparko thought, I'm being paranoid, but it looked as though Coral had spoken to Carrots, who was still busy being the DJ. Sparko wouldn't have put it past her . . . as soon as she and Julian hit the dance floor, the smoochy stuff began, oozing out of the sound system like treacle. Quick as a flash, they were glued together. She had her arms round his neck, and her body blended into his. He wasn't objecting. Sparko could imagine the effect this position must have been having on poor old glamour-puss Philips. He seemed quite dazed when the music stopped. Sparko looked over to where Louise had been standing. Opinion was divided about her. Was she his girlfriend or wasn't she? They were usually together. Was she pretty or not? Skinny or elegant? Mousy or quiet? One thing was quite clear to Sparko: she was miserable. One minute she was looking as though she were about to burst into tears, and the next time he glanced over at her she'd gone, and all her pals had gone with her. Off to the loo, no doubt, which seemed to be where girls spent most of the time whenever they went to discos. She's a fool, Sparko thought. Why has she let Coral just come in and snatch Julian away like that? Why didn't she do something? *Oh, yes, clever clogs, like what, exactly? The same kind of thing you did when Julian swept Coral out of the room to . . . wherever he did sweep her off to. Didn't come back for ages and ages, did they?*

76

and it doesn't exactly take an Einstein to work out that they weren't discussing European agricultural policy . . . and what did you do about it, big brave Sparko? Nothing. Zilch. Zero. Nada. You are some kind of a hero. Give yourself a medal.

No sooner had they come back, than they'd left. Coral had the grace to come and say goodbye to him. She whispered, "Tell you all about it, kiddo," and off she'd gone, arm-in-arm with the Hunk.

Now here he was, all alone.

"Nobody loves me!" Sparko muttered to himself, and began to do a little dance of sadness all along the pavement. "That's the last disco I'm ever going to, ever."

BATHTIME
Sparko

Sparko loved showering, but today was an exception. He loved singing at the top of his voice, but today the only words in his head were "I don't care", so he tried to fit them to various tunes, and found that they worked very well with "Unchained Melody". And he *didn't* care. Not really. Let Coral run off with that stuffed shirt, Julian. No skin off his nose. He hoped very much that she'd be miserable, but feared the worst. She would probably manage to be ecstatically happy. She usually did. "I don't care!" he sang at the top of his voice. His not caring extended to whether he woke the Flintstone Brothers or not. Too bad if he did. Normally, on a Sunday, there was no danger of attack from that direction. They sank into their beds late on a Saturday night and came to next day only with great difficulty when the roasted meat smells coming from the kitchen reached their noses. How his mother managed to get what she called "a proper Sunday dinner" on the table every week, considering what she had to do in the pub, was a mystery, but there it was, every time: some poor little farmyard creature, basted and roasted and tucked up cosily in a nest of golden potatoes, with something green on the side. Sparko had been begging off Sunday dinner for years, and today he had a really good excuse. He was going over to Dweebsie's house for a script conference. Part of him sort of wanted to hear that Lydia had given Dweebsie the coldest of shoulders, but he recognised, even in his miserable state, that this was mean and unkind, so he made a big effort and tried to hope that his friend had found happiness in her arms . . . or at least had managed to make his way down into them from the towering heights which he generally inhabited.

Whatever, they had to have some kind of a script. Improvisation was all very nice and fine, but everyone felt more secure when they had a wodge of paper in their hands and proper lines to learn. It wasn't long now before the end of term. Only four weeks until the show, and they didn't even have a title. He hoped that Dweebsie was feeling creative. Poor old Sparko, he told himself, all you can think about is Coral. How sad is that! He tried to concentrate instead on the problem of Mary's song for the last act. He'd almost finished it now, but was it any good? And would

Lydia be able to sing it? He didn't even know what sort of sound she made, but he knew exactly what he wanted: an ethereal, other-worldly quality; a sort of thinner, higher, more dreamlike noise than most people could manage, but one that wispy old Lydia might just have quite naturally, if he was lucky. Her speaking voice was right. Would she sound the same when she sang? Sparko closed his eyes and put his head under the hot water. I wish, he thought, I could stay here all day.

REHEARSAL
SATURDAY 20 NOVEMBER, 1999

10.00 a.m. Act One. Principals and Dancers

2.00 p.m. Chorus and Dancers

BALLET STUDIO

PLEASE BE PUNCTUAL!!

If I wasn't too caught up with Julian, Coral thought, I might consider Mickey Flannery. It annoyed her to admit it, but he was exactly right for a modern-day Joseph . . . skinny and blue-eyed, with very pale skin and very black hair. He looked as Irish as his name, and there were some moods in which a dreamy, poetic-type person appealed to Coral. She said as much to Pammy, who had to come in for all rehearsals, poor thing, because she was doing stage management.

"He's OK, isn't he, Mickey? Who's he going out with?"

"I don't know. Maybe no one. This'll be news to you, but some people are not as obsessed with all that sort of thing as you are."

"Rubbish. They are. They just keep it hidden, that's all. Anyway, I don't care. I've got Julian."

"So you have. How could I possibly have forgotten? How's things? Hot and sweaty? Torrid and breathless? Tell me all . . ."

Coral opened her mouth, but before she could say anything Nish had clapped his hands, and all the dancers, Coral included, had to stop what they were doing and go up on stage. She sighed. It wasn't that she minded going through the routine eighty-eight times, but she wished they could have started a little later. She'd hardly had time for breakfast, even. It had been a question of either washing her hair or eating, and shampooing won, as it always did. Now at least she looked better than any of the rest of them, even though her stomach was beginning to make growling, feed-me sort of noises. Fortunately, the tape was nice and loud and what with that and the thumping of fifteen pairs of feet on the wooden stage, no one was going to hear it.

Nish said: "Right, girls, you first. You resent this new person who's just come in . . . she's been given a better room than you've got . . . and she hasn't even had her baby. There are some of you in this B&B who can't turn round in your room because of kids under your feet. Lydia, you must be a little scared, but basically too caught up in your own problems to worry about them much . . . they're taking out their anger on the landlord, mainly. OK, let's go . . . from the top."

Coral followed the others as they launched into the number called "Who Does She Think She Is?" The chorus weren't coming in until the afternoon – late lie-in for them, lucky things – so Sparko was saying the words to the rhythm of the music, which was fair enough as he'd written them:

"Who does she think she is, eh?
Coming in here, bold as brass,
Not a penny to her name.
Talk about the underclass!
She is lowering the tone.
(You know us. We never moan.)
Why should she have
What we don't have?
Who does she think?
Who does she think?
Who does she think she is, eh?"

Nish said: "That's good. OK, once more from the top, and, Lydia, I want you to look more scared. You're not used to having all this aggro from people. And Joseph isn't here to protect you for the moment . . . you're all on your own. Look terrified."

The scenery was still being painted: nothing elaborate, just a couple of flats, which were enormous wooden and canvas things, painted on one side to be the B&B and on the other to be the street at night. Lydia cowered against the chair that had been put there until the flat was ready. It wasn't hard pretending to be scared: she really, truly was. She came to every rehearsal convinced that something would have changed: she wouldn't be able to transform.

That was what she called it in her own head: the strange process that she didn't understand at all, but which happened when she said Mary's words aloud. It was, Lydia thought, a bit like being a werewolf, but less hairy. She changed, but she was always nervous that next time the magic would be gone. She wanted so much to tell Sparko about it, because she was sure he'd understand. He, too, changed, whenever he danced. All the music was now on tape, and whenever the machine was switched on you could see the sound, almost, travelling along his arms and legs and making him strong, and graceful, and taller than he really was. It made him hold his head differently. It made him lighter. He could jump, and spring, and turn, and move as silently as breath. There was one bit of the show Lydia liked especially, and that was the tiny little dance Sparko did with Nish, right in the middle of the opening "Town at Night" scene. They were two drunks going home together, propping one another up as they staggered across the stage, and every single time they did it, whoever happened to be watching burst into spontaneous applause: they looked so funny, as though they hadn't got a single bone in their bodies but were made of rubber.

Dweebsie was looking at her. He waved from the back of the studio which was where he was sitting today. She smiled back. She didn't dare raise her hand to wave. That would have been out of character . . . that was what they called it when she became Lydia while she was supposed to be Mary. Dweebsie . . . she felt a little guilty about him. Walking back from the disco the other night was exciting. She'd never been alone with a boy before, in the dark, and walking through the cold night streets. Dweebsie took her hand as they'd left school and didn't let go of it all the way home. He'd talked a lot: much more than he normally did, and so had she. Dweebsie was easy to talk to. But he knew, and she knew, that at the end of the walk something would have to happen. He'd try to kiss her. Lydia knew he would. Would she mind? Should she let him? That would mean they were going out together, wouldn't it? Did she want to go out with Dweebsie? Would she know how to kiss properly? She'd only kissed two people before, and that wasn't really properly. Her heart was thumping as they approached the gate.

"This is where I live," she said quietly.

"Oh, right!" Dweebsie came to a complete standstill, and

turned to her. Lydia wished the ground would open up and swallow her . . . this was *soooo* embarrassing! What should she say? What would he do? She closed her eyes, so that she wouldn't have to think about it, and found herself folded in Dweebsie's arms, with her head squashed up against his chest. He was so tall! She struggled for air, and turned her face up to him . . .

"Dweebsie . . . I can't breathe," she said.

"Nor me," he said.

"Why not? Why can't you breathe?"

"Because . . . you take my breath away." He grinned at her. "It's true. Can I kiss you, Lydia?"

She couldn't bring herself to answer, so she nodded, closed her eyes and opened her mouth, and then they were kissing and everything was OK.

Later on, in bed, Lydia had wondered what they would say to one another next time they met, but as that turned out to be at a rehearsal, everything was normal, and what she said was "Hi" and his answer had been "Hi" as well. So that was all right.

"OK, everyone, break for food," said Nish. "That's much better. We're doing all the songs at two o'clock, so guard those voices. No yelling."

Everyone gathered their stuff together and made a rush for the door.

Nish turned to Sparko and said: "What's with Mary's last song? You done yet?"

"Almost," said Sparko. "I'll let you see it on Monday. I'm just putting the finishing touches. You know."

"It better be good, man," said Nish. "You've been long enough writing it."

"It's not as though I haven't got anything else to do, though, is it? I'm just a dogsbody around here, that's all. Anything need doing, ask Sparko, right?"

"Right," said Nish. "And you love it. Don't pretend you don't."

They both jumped off the stage and followed the rest of the company out of the door. Café Lucia was a no-no by now . . . every table would be taken. They'd have to go looking for somewhere else.

Telephone conversation:

Sparko and Dweebsie,

21 November 1999, 11.30 p.m.

Dweebsie: But what I want to know is, how can you tell?

Sparko: From the way they behave, I suppose. I don't know, Dweeb. Why don't you ask someone else?

D: I wouldn't. I wouldn't talk to anyone else about this kind of stuff.

S: Thank you very much, I don't think. What have I done to you to get all this spilling-out-your-heart routine?

D: I've known you for ever. I'm not embarrassed to say things like that to you . . .

S: Lucky old me, eh?

D: I really like her, Sparko. You know?

S: I do know. Dream about her every night, break out in a hot sweat every time you see her, heart beats faster, etc., etc.

D: Right! Right! I knew I should talk to you.

S: But what do you need me to tell you? That's what I can't understand.

D (*sighing*): Concentrate, Sparks! I want to know how I know if she really, really likes me.

S: When you're kissing her. . . I assume you *are* kissing her. . .

D: Yeah. Go on, what when I'm kissing her?

S: Does she go all kind of soft and, well, relaxed? Does she seem to be enjoying it?

D: Yeah, yeah. She does. Yeah.

S: You don't sound too sure.

D: Of course I'm sure . . . yeah. Sure I am.

S: Then it's OK. Trust me. As long as she isn't pushing you away and going all cold on you, that's fine.

D: Sure?

S: Yes . . . Dweeb, I've got to get some sleep, man. Go to bed. Dream of Lydia.

D: Right! Thanks a lot, Sparko . . . 'night.

S: Yeah, night-night, lover-boy.

ACT TWO, FINALE

Rehearsal for EVERYONE
at 3.30 p.m.
Monday 22 Nov. 1999
(including dancers, walk-ons
and backstage staff)

It wasn't working out. At first Lydia thought that having a boyfriend would change everything. She'd feel grown-up; everyone would accept her because Dweebsie was so popular; no one would be jealous, because they didn't reckon he was one of the school hunks – everything should have been perfect. But it wasn't. Lydia sat at the back of the class while Slender Sam, the English teacher, droned on and on at the front about *Twelfth Night*, which they had just started studying. That was part of the problem. Shakespeare was a bit scary. It was one thing to thrill to Gwyneth Paltrow and the delicious Joseph Fiennes in the movie about him being in love, but that was just a movie, and once you looked at all those words on the page they swam about before your eyes and didn't make sense. They almost did, but not quite. Reading them was like looking at a message in a kind of code: you got some parts of it and missed others. Slender Sam was trying to be reassuring.

"It all looks desperately unfamiliar now, of course, but trust me. Trust me, and let yourselves be carried along by the glorious verse, and I promise you you'll love it, all of you, by the time you have to answer questions on it."

Lydia sighed. That was enough to take the fun out of most things. She found it hard to imagine that she ever *would* learn to love the words, but, sure as eggs were eggs, doing exams on them wasn't going to help. She tuned out Slender Sam and went back to thinking about Dweebsie. In her rough book, which was open in front of her, she drew a line down the middle of one page, and on one side of the line she wrote the good things about him, and on the other the things she was worried about. She studied both sides and sighed. He was kind, and clever, and quite handsome. He didn't smell, which was brilliant (because she had discovered that lots of boys thought showers were only for very special occasions), he took her to the movies, he sometimes paid for her drinks at the Café Lucia, and (this was the best thing about him) he didn't put any pressure on her at all to go the whole way. Lydia would never have confessed this to anyone, but she was quite scared of someone she really liked saying they wanted to make love to her. She wasn't sure about many things, but she was quite sure about this. The whole idea filled her with a kind of dread. She'd thought of writing to an agony aunt about it but was too embarrassed. Once, she'd asked her mum about it, in a general kind of way, after the papers had been full of the story of a thirteen-year-old girl who had given birth to a baby. Her mum was quite firm about it. The age of consent, she told Lydia, was there for a reason. You're not ready before that for all the grown-up emotions, and so on and so on. After that, Lydia felt a bit better, but it hadn't really been a problem then, and it didn't look as though Dweebsie was intending to make it one. It occurred to Lydia while she was busy making her list that maybe boys got just as nervous about sex as girls did, but she couldn't really ask him. Anyway, most girls didn't seem nervous at all. Some of them even boasted about what they did with their boyfriends. She glanced over to where Coral was sitting. Ever since she'd snatched Julian Philips from under poor Louise's nose at the disco, she'd been prancing around like a cat who'd just swallowed a tasty canary. I'll bet, Lydia thought, that *they* go all the way. Julian wouldn't be like Dweebsie about sex. So why was she looking so gloomy now? She had been unusually silent, for Coral. Perhaps it was what Slender Sam was saying. Lydia tuned in briefly:

". . . about the possibility of love, and the ridiculousness of it, and the way, as Feste the clown puts it, that 'the whirligig of time brings in his revenges'. Who knows what that means?"

Lydia knew whose hand would go up and it did. Good old Dweebsie! He was really into Shakespeare and all sorts of difficult books. He would have been quite happy to curl up on a sofa reading all day. He'd told her so once, as though this were a guilty secret. Now he said: "It means that if you wait long enough, things that need sorting out will get sorted. The baddies will get their comeuppance. Eventually. That sort of thing."

Slender Sam smiled. "Quite right, Matthew, if not expressed in the most elegant of language."

Slender Sam was very keen on elegance of language and Lydia realised that it must sometimes be quite depressing for him to have them to cope with every day. He'd started out in life as an actor. You could see that, just by looking at him, but he did keep talking about it as well . . . the time he was in this play at this theatre . . . the way Sir someone or other told him to read this or that speech. It was a bit tragic, really. She turned her attention to her Dweebsie list again. He liked her, he truly did. She could tell. He was clever. The list of all the things that were good about going out with him was long; there wasn't any way of getting over that. In the opposite column there were only two items, but the way

Lydia looked at it, there was no way of getting round what they said. The first was *I don't fancy him* and the second, the really damning one, was *He isn't Sparko*. She sighed and listened as Dweebsie started reading from the play:

> *"If music be the food of love, play on.*
> *Give me excess of it, that, surfeiting,*
> *The appetite may sicken, and so die . . ."*

Lydia blinked and looked down at the text in front of her. *What* was all that about?

Coral was in a foul mood. She sat at the back of the hall, watching them all prancing about to Sparko's music in the dance that came just before the final curtain. The Christmas show had a title now, and in Coral's opinion it was the naffest thing since . . . the last naff thing . . . she couldn't even be bothered to think of anything. Hideous, that was what it was. Who in their right mind would want to see something called *Light a Candle*?. The song that went with it wasn't too bad, at least when Sparko had played it to her on his guitar and sung the words. OK, OK, it was really sad and tears had come into her eyes, but that might just have been Sparko. What was the betting Lydia would wreck it? Could she sing? Had anyone heard her? She was learning the thing, apparently, and would let them all hear it at the next rehearsal.

Dweebsie was teaching her . . . poor old Lydia! It was quite clear to Coral that even though she was supposed to be going out with the Dweeb, little Lydia still yearned for old Sparko. And Sparko still wanted no one but her, Coral. And she was meant to be passionately in love with Julian . . . how could she ever admit to anyone that he wasn't turning out to be all that he was supposed to be? She tried very hard not even to admit it to herself . . . it had been such a triumph, waltzing out of that silly disco with him slavering away beside her. And since then, she'd been able to sit with the Year Twelves and go about with them, and even once or twice, pass as eighteen in a pub.

She didn't really enjoy it, although this, too, she would never have admitted to anyone. What if someone who knew her came in? Or, worse still, someone who knew her mum, who seemed to be acquainted with half the town? If word got back that Coral had been seen in a pub, she might as well ground herself for the foreseeable future and have done with it. She'd been careful not to drink anything alcoholic, but still. She'd been on pins the whole evening, and not in the mood for snogging when Julian walked her home. Normally, there was nothing she enjoyed more than kissing and cuddling, but this was getting heavy and difficult. Julian was nearly eighteen. He was doing his best to persuade her that there was nothing wrong with sex at her age. She'd been able, by using a set of half-truths, to hold him off so far, but how much longer would he wait? Was she going to have to give in, after all? Coral knew very well that most people thought she'd been all the way with lots of boys. It was part of her image. The truth was a bit different. It wasn't that she thought it was wrong, necessarily, but she was nervous of all sorts of things she'd never told anyone about: pregnancy, and diseases, and she didn't like the idea of filling her body with chemicals and taking the contraceptive pill. As far as she was concerned, she wanted admiration and attention and a lot of snogging. That would do her nicely for a bit, until she was older. So what was she supposed to do about Julian?

The worst thing of all was not having a single person she could talk to. Suddenly, the awfulness of everything came over her: the Julian problem, the fact that she had such a measly part in this stupid play with the naff name, and her Science homework, which had to be done by tomorrow and which she still hadn't looked at. She felt tears filling her eyes, and stood up. They couldn't see her crying. They mustn't. She ran out of the room towards the cloakroom.

"Let's not go to Lucia," Coral said. "They'll all be there, with their eyes out on stalks. Nosy devils."

"You can't blame them," said Lydia. "They're worried about you. You can come to my house if you like."

"Really? Thanks. OK. That'd be good."

The two girls walked along in silence. A few flakes of snow were trying to make it down from the sky but turning into sleet before they reached the pavement. Lydia didn't really know what to say to Coral, now that the worst was over. When she'd found her weeping in the cloakroom, she'd known exactly what to do. She'd put her arms around Coral, and said things like "It's OK" (when it obviously wasn't) and "Don't cry . . . it can't be that bad" (when it clearly was), which were really stupid and yet which seemed to cheer Coral up. At any rate, she'd stopped crying and followed Lydia willingly out of school. And now they were going home to Lydia's house like old friends. Lydia couldn't help feeling good about this, and she wondered if it was OK to be happy when the person you were supposed to be helping was feeling so sad. She'll come up to my room, Lydia thought, and maybe she'll tell me what's wrong.

"This is really nice of you," Coral said, sniffing, but more like her normal self. And when she smiled at Lydia, it was like the sun coming out.

Telephone conversation:
Coral and Sparko,
27 November 1999, 12.30 p.m.

Coral: Are you doing something? Is it OK to talk?

Sparko: Of course I'm doing something. You didn't seriously think I was just sitting here by the phone waiting for you to call, did you?

C: What *are* you doing? Go on, tell me. Is it anything interesting?

S: It is to you. I'm doing your homework. Well, my homework, but I have to do it early so that you can copy it, remember? Ring any bells?

C: You're a treasure, Sparko. I don't know what I'd do without you. Thank you!

S: Mention it!

(*Laughter from Coral. This is a very old joke, going back to Year Seven.*)

C: Can you listen to this, though? I've got something to tell you. I've made a decision.

S: Let's hear it, then.

C: I'm breaking up with Jules . . . Why aren't you saying anything?

S: Is it possible? The girl of my dreams has finally seen the light . . . there is a chance for me . . . be still, my beating heart! Just hold on a mo while I do a tap-dance for sheer joy . . .

C: Be serious, Sparko . . .

S: I am . . . I am being serious. This is a joyous day for me . . .

C: I don't see why . . .

S: You can go out with me now. I will lay the world at your feet for you to walk on . . .

C: Give over, and listen for a minute instead of wittering on. How am I going to do it?

S: Do what?

C: Tell Jules, of course.

S: Why are you asking me? What's happened to the Gossip Queens? Doesn't Pammy have any ideas?

C (*sighing*): Everyone says to do something different. Pammy says phone, Shushila says write, but Lydia says I should tell him face to face. I don't fancy doing that.

S: Since when has Lydia been one of the gang? I've missed something . . .

C: She's OK, Lydia.

S: I know that. I told *you* that!

C: We're not supposed to be talking about Lydia. We're talking about me.

S (*whispering*): As usual.

C: What was that?

S: Nothing. Go on.

C: I heard you!

S: Then why did you ask?

C: Stick to the point, Sparko. What do *you* think I should do?

S: I think you should tell him face to face. Then come

round here and get up close and personal with me. Your Science homework is nearly finished . . . I'll be waiting.

C: You're mad, you are! See you!

S: Where are you going?

C: Shopping. I need a chucking Julian outfit.

S: I give up. Bye.

C: I love you, really . . . bye. (*Puts phone down.*)

S: I wish . . . (*Puts phone down and runs hand sadly through hair. Turns to homework.*)

Sparko sometimes wished he had the kind of hair that you could tear. It would come in very useful on occasions like this. It just hadn't been his day. He should have stayed in bed and skipped straight from Thursday to Saturday, leaving out this Friday, which even though it was missing the one, was turning out in every other respect to be exactly like a Friday the thirteenth. It all started when he got to school. Coral was lying in wait for him in reception, and like a fool he'd been pleased.

"Come on," she said. "Where have you been?"

"Why, what's the matter?"

"It's Katie. She wants to see both of us. Do you think this could be IT?"

Sparko knew what she was on about without any further explanation. For the last two days Coral had talked about nothing else. She didn't care at all about poor old Julian Philips mooching round the school with navy-blue bags under his eyes; she didn't care about the rude names the Year Twelves were calling her in solidarity with their favourite hunk: all she could think about was Northside TV and when they were going to let them know the results of the audition. For his part, Sparko had almost forgotten about "Muesli Mews".

There was too much else to worry about. The songs for the show were written and were mostly being sung as he meant them to be, but there was a problem with the last number: the title song, "Light a Candle". Lydia was supposed to sing it, and she'd been making all kinds of excuses every time they came to rehearse it. The bits for the chorus were fine, but the verses . . . today was the day when he would tackle Lydia. She couldn't keep on avoiding him for ever. He'd come to the conclusion, just from looking at how they were when they were together, that all was not well between her and Dweebsie. He should ask Dweebsie, he supposed, but somehow they always talked about other things whenever they met, which wasn't very often these days, what with wall-to-wall rehearsals. How come girls always managed to find time to natter? And how come girls always spoke about the innermost secrets of their hearts as soon as look at you? I'll do it, Sparko decided. I'll talk to Dweebsie . . . only not today. Today was the music rehearsal, and that was the most important thing. He realised suddenly that he still hadn't answered Coral, so he said:

"Could be, I suppose. Don't know."

"Well, don't look so excited about it. Come on, she's waiting for us."

Coral knocked on the head's door.

"Come in!" Katie G. called out, and in they went.

When they came out, Coral was walking about six inches off the ground with happiness, and Sparko was dragging along behind her. She kept saying: "Oh, Sparko . . . you don't mind? Truly and really? Only I'm so happy! Imagine! Me on the telly . . . isn't it great?"

Sparko made all the right noises. He *didn't* really care. He was a dancer. He was a musician. He was not a bit-part actor in a soap. Never in a million years. And yet . . . it hurt in a way he didn't quite recognise. He'd gone in for something and failed. *It's the first time*, he realised with a shock, the very first time in the whole of his fifteen years that he'd gone in for something and not got it. If this was a movie, he thought, this would be the dark before the storm. The little disaster before the final triumph. Think Tom Cruise . . .

He tried to be happy for Coral. Correction: he *was* happy for Coral. And at least with Coral involved in the soap, he'd be involved as well. If he wanted to be. Coral was talking and talking . . . about the dates they'd be filming (sixth and seventh of January, as if he gave a damn). He knew that the only way to stop her was to pay her a compliment. He said: "It doesn't matter how small the part is, you'll still be brilliant."

A kiss on the cheek was his reward. It was the first nice thing to happen since he'd woken up, and, though he didn't know it at the time, the last as well.

Sparko was rapidly losing patience. He said: "No, no, no . . . it's not supposed to be a dirge, for heaven's sake. It's poignant but joyful, got it? It's hopeful. It's moving. It should bring tears to the eyes, but not depress the audience. Get it? The baby that's just been born . . . well, OK, we're not saying in so many words it's the Baby Jesus, but that's what the story's been about, hasn't it? No one's going to think of it as anything other than a modern Nativity, in spite of all the things we've done with it. Right. Let's take it from the top."

Sparko waved his arm, and the two guitarists began to play. The drummer swished about in the background. Sparko turned to the piano and began to pick out the tune. The chorus, who were squashed into the studio, began singing again.

"That's more like it," Sparko said when they'd finished. "Now, where's Lydia?"

"Here I am," said Lydia, detaching herself from the radiator, which she'd been hugging.

"Come on, then, Lydia. Let's have the solo verse."

"Must I?"

"Yes," said Sparko gently. "You must. You're Mary, remember? This is your lullaby to your baby."

"But I can't really sing."

"I'll be the judge of that. Go on."

Lydia walked to the piano with the air of someone going to an execution. She began singing in (almost) the right place, and there was nothing particularly bad about how she did it, but . . . but, but, but . . . All the magic that she brought to her spoken words was missing somehow, and Sparko doubted whether there was anything they could do. He'd have to talk to Dweebsie about it. He looked over to where his friend was sitting with his head in his hands.

"Thanks, Lydia," he said, when she'd finished singing. He tried to think of something else to say, but nothing occurred to him. This was a serious problem. To his complete astonishment, Lydia put her hand over her mouth and burst into tears. At once, all the girls in the room rushed to her side and made a kind of wall around her. Sparko stood up from the piano, and Dweebsie uncurled and went to see if he could help. As usual, while they were all faffing about,

Coral took control. Sometimes it seemed to Sparko that she was exactly like her deputy head of a mother.

"Give her a bit of space," Coral was saying, and to Lydia: "Don't cry, Lydia. It's fine. I'll do it. Really. It'll be fine."

"What d'you mean, you'll do it?" Dweebsie had found his tongue. "It's Mary's song . . . you aren't even on stage at this point."

"I can come on, can't I? I can be . . . I don't know . . . an angel or something . . . a figment of Mary's imagination. What does it matter?"

"But can you do the song?" Sparko asked, and was rewarded with a look that would have curdled milk at ten paces.

"Let's see, shall we?" Coral leaned on the piano as though she was about to sing a raunchy nightclub song, not a touching lullaby. Sparko's heart filled with dread. How was he going to break the news to her that she was not right for what was needed? Anita in *West Side Story* was one thing. Or shimmying like my sister Kate . . . this was quite another. He took a deep breath and began to play. Coral started to sing, and Sparko's hands nearly slid off the keys. Where had she found this voice? It soared up from her mouth and every note hung in the air like a pearl, like a tear-drop: pure and silvery and true. Every word was clear, every note exactly right, every rise and fall of the lyric heartbreakingly lovely. Sparko found tears coming into his eyes, and he blinked them away. She sounded . . . she sounded not like Coral, but like some disembodied voice, the voice of an angel. When she finished singing, there was total silence in the studio. Dweebsie was stunned. Lydia had started crying all over again, and the others were totally gobsmacked.

"There you go," said Coral into the silence. "What did I tell you? Angelic or what?"

"More than angelic. Seraphic. Transcendent," said Sparko, bounding up from the piano stool to hug her. "I think you've just saved the Christmas show."

Telephone conversation:
Lydia and Coral,
15 December 1999, 8.00 p.m.

Lydia: How can you be so calm? It's only three days to the show. What if I forget my words? What if it's awful, and everyone hates it? Well, *you* won't be awful. You'll be brilliant. You're always brilliant, and you're never nervous.

Coral: I am, of course I am. But you have to be. Didn't you know? If you aren't nervous, there's something wrong . . . you'll be flat and terrible. It's the feeling awful that gets you kind of ready to perform. Really. Tatty always says that. She says *ze throat it is dry and ze heart he is in ze mouth.*

L (*giggling*): You always cheer me up. Are you all right?

C: What do you mean? Why on earth shouldn't I be?

L: Oh, help! I shouldn't have said anything . . . I thought you knew . . .

C: Knew what? What haven't you told me? Go on, you've got to say now . . . you can't keep quiet.

L: It's Julian. I heard Nish tell Sparko . . . I don't think I was meant to hear . . . I heard him tell Sparko that Julian said you were frigid.

C: (*Silence.*)

L: Are you there? Did you hear? Coral? Are you OK?

C: I'm fine, but that Julian'd better watch out. He's not the only one who can go round spreading rumours. He won't be able to show his face by the time I've finished with him.

L: Why? What're you going to do?

C (chuckling): Wait and see . . . Julian's reputation's going to be in shreds by the time I've finished with him. And look . . . I've stopped you worrying about the show, haven't I?

L: You've reminded me again . . . oh, God. What'll I do if I forget all my words?

C (sighing): Here we go again . . .

Redgate Academy Christmas Show '99

LIGHT A CANDLE

Devised by Matthew Deebles and the company
Directed by Warren Nash
Choreography and music by Simon Parks
Stage management by Pamela Norrington

Mary . . . Lydia Stevenson
Joseph . . . Mickey Flannery
Landlord . . . Warren Nash
The Angel . . . Coral de Barros

B&B clients, townspeople, etc . . .
members of Years 10 and 11

18 and 19 December
7.30 p.m.

At exactly seven o'clock, Pammy stuck her head round the door of the girls' dressing-room and said in a voice like something out of "Doctor Who": "Ladies, this is your half-hour call! Half an hour, please."

"Who do you think you are?" said Coral, laughing. She was standing behind Lydia, trying to persuade her that without a bit of brown eyebrow pencil she'd look completely dreadful, but they both stopped arguing to laugh at Pammy.

"I'm the tannoy . . . the electronic announcement system, you know, that tells you when to go on stage, etc. Just one of the perks of being stage management. Break a leg, ladies."

She was gone. Lydia said: "But I'm Mary. I'm supposed to be kind of ethereal, aren't I?"

"Ethereal is one thing. Totally invisible is quite another. Sit still while I do your eyes."

The girls' dressing-room was crowded. Redgate didn't run to private dressing-rooms, but this one was enormous, and there were showers and best of all, as far as Coral was concerned, the mirrors had lightbulbs all round them. That made it like a proper theatre. Lydia gazed at the palette of coloured sticks spread out in front of her. She'd brought in a bit of lipstick and some powder, but Coral had swept those back into her bag, and said: "Leave it to me. It's clear you don't know the first thing about make-up."

Lydia watched them from the wings. There they were, her friends, dancing on stage, completely changed by costume and make-up. They moved in the ways they'd been rehearsing for ages, but somehow, with the lights shining down on them, and the music booming, amplified, all around them, everything was different. She felt cold with fear. Soon, she and Mickey would have to go out there. The lights would shine in her eyes, and that meant that she couldn't see the audience, but she'd know they were there: watching her, listening to her. What if she stayed Lydia? What if she didn't remember the words? Here was Mickey. He was taking her hand. They were on. They were there, actually on the stage. Lydia blinked. Oh, help! she thought, and glanced across the stage, to where Sparko and Nish were nearing the end of their silly drunken dance. Then the scenery vanished, and the auditorium might as well have been on Mars. Her feet hurt. Her heart ached. Where would they sleep? The snow was coming down. Mickey was speaking. Not Mickey. Joseph. Speaking to her.

"Let's try, eh, Mary? Can you make it as far as that corner? Someone told me there was a bed and breakfast we could try. Just a bit further. Honest. It'll be OK. Right?"

And she followed him. She spoke to him. It was going to be all right. Lydia had gone. In her place was Mary.

Nick and Pete, Sparko's brothers, had been made to come to the Christmas show as usual. They were resentful and cross. Sparko never came to see them in matches. Sparko never had to do anything he didn't want to do. It wasn't fair.

"Life isn't fair," their mother had said. "I want support for our

Simon and that's the last word on the subject. Otherwise you two are grounded. That's it. And no pocket money either while I'm about it. And if you breathe a word to Simon that I've made you come, I'll tear you both limb from limb."

That was rich, coming from their tiny little mum, but both boys knew better than to cross her when she meant business. And at least this year it hadn't been as bad as they'd feared. No tutus. No soppy Christmas carols. Quite fit girls wearing normal-type clothes, and the music was OK too. Their mother had pointed to the programme and shown them.

"Something to be grateful for," Pete had muttered. "At least if he's in charge of the other dancers, he won't be prancing around himself."

There was one dance he did, though, where he was being a drunk, along with that black kid. That was cool.

Coral went through the steps with all the others before the first-act finale. So far so good. Nothing had gone particularly wrong, though there was a sticky moment when Nish had opened the door of the B&B and nearly brought the flat down round his head. He'd improvised brilliantly and said something about the place falling to bits and needing repair, but it was a narrow shave. And it came just before Lydia's outburst. Not a dry eye in the house. It was strange: being up there on stage and feeling the emotion coming back at you from the audience. Laughter was obvious, but this was something else. You could practically touch the sadness whooshing up from everyone sitting there. Coral was leaning against the wall at that point, so she could sneak a look at what was happening in the audience, and there were plenty of hankies being taken out, and plenty of eyes being wiped. Amazing. She could see Dweebsie standing in the wings, gazing at Lydia with his mouth open. He was so sweet . . . she'd have to have a word with Lydia. It looked to her as though the whole relationship was a bit one-sided. But I, she thought triumphantly, forgetting all about Dweebsie and Lydia, have done it. My name *is* on the programme, after all. Not one of the odds and sods, but up there with the principals. Just because of my voice. I'm the Angel. Sparko had changed the words around a little and now the song was hers: the song that everyone would remember. The one they'd go out humming. The one that would stay with them. The hit. Her song. Roll on act two!

This is it, Sparko thought. The crunch. He'd done everything he could now. He wasn't on in this last scene, so he could watch it from the wings, with Dweebsie. This was the bit that was going to knock them out: the bringing of the gifts from all the people in the B&B; the ones who'd been so horrible to Mary and Joseph when they first came, but who now brought food and clothes and stuff for the baby, and then Coral, whose gift was a candle. She came in last of all, when the others were gathered round the crib, which was just a drawer out of a chest of drawers.

"*It's not much,*" she said in her Angel's voice. "*But it's pretty, and if you put it in the window it'll shine out so that everyone can see it.*"

"*Thanks,*" said Lydia being Mary, moved by everyone's kindness. "*It's lovely.*"

And then the lights dimming and the music coming in, soft at first, and the whole company singing:

>*"Light a candle for the baby,*
>*Light a candle for the boy,*
>*Set a candle in the window*
>*To bring comfort, love and joy."*

Then Coral, kneeling by the crib, with the lighted candle in her hand throwing shadows on her face and making her beautiful in a way she had never been beautiful before, and as she opened her mouth to sing, a silence you could touch and feel spreading through the hall:

>*"Sleep, my baby,*
>*Sleep my love.*
>*Angels sing*
>*A lullaby.*

Stars shine down
From high above.
Sweetest baby,
Never cry.
Here's a candle.
Watch the light
Shining out
Pure and bright,
Spreading gold
Through the night."

And then the chorus again. And then the curtain. The end. Sparko found that he, too, had tears in his eyes. The applause was deafening. The curtain was pulled back again and again, and they took their bows as the clapping went on and on. As he made his way to the front of the stage with Nish and the Dweeb for a round of applause all on their own, he caught sight of his mother. Predictably enough, she had tears pouring down her cheeks, but his brothers . . . well, wonders would never cease. Their Neanderthal hearts had clearly been touched. They were both smiling. They were clapping along with everyone else.

"You're Mrs de Barros, aren't you? I'm Lydia Stevenson's mum . . . Annabel. Your daughter was wonderful . . . such a beautiful voice."

"And yours was wonderful as well. They've grown quite friendly over the rehearsal period, haven't they? I'm for ever hearing Lydia this and Lydia that . . . it's good to meet you. And do call me Susan. Mrs de Barros sounds too teacherish for words. How are you finding it up here after London?"

Coral's mother and Lydia's mother went on chatting as they made their way backstage to congratulate their daughters.

Crowds of people had come in to say how good they were. Even Julian, with Louise on his arm, had found some kind things to say. Looking at them, Coral remembered that she was supposed to be spreading ghastly rumours about him all over the school . . . she'd forgotten all about her revenge in the excitement of the last few days' rehearsals. She decided that she was going to be dead nice and let bygones be bygones.

When that crowd had gone, Katie the Great, Slender Sam, Tatty and even Mr Whitely had all trooped in to congratulate the company. Katie G. had summed it all up: "We're very proud of you," she said. "You are, all of you, a credit to Redgate."

Coral smeared make-up removing cream over her face and peered into the mirror. There he was, the invisible interviewer. She spoke to him in her head, because there were so many people about: *It's the first time I've sung anything like that, it's true, but I do believe it's a direction I want to explore . . .*

She was going to spend her Christmas money on CDs. More of Lesley Garrett, and someone called Kiri Te Kanawa, who was gorgeous . . . she knew most of the best songs by female pop stars of the last few years by heart, but there was so much more to learn . . . and fancy Lydia's mum being so smart and pretty! Lydia was staying over tonight, so that they could go into school together tomorrow . . .

Lydia was sitting by herself at the dressing-table. The bulbs round the mirrors had been turned off now, and in the overhead strip lighting her skin looked grey and pale.

They'd all gone now: Mum and Coral's mum who'd come in and kissed them and shrieked about how brilliant they were; Sparko's mum; Sparko's two brothers, who weren't like cavemen at all, but quite sweet. They'd both come up to her and muttered about how good the show was, and then shuffled off again. And Sparko had hugged her. Really hugged her. She was still getting over that. And Nish had hugged her. Everyone had hugged everyone else. They'd be in Café Lucia and keeping a place for her. Coral had promised. Lydia wanted to be alone for a bit, just to remember what it had all been like; to go over everything in her head. Some of it was terrifying. That second when you came on to the stage and before you knew what was going to happen . . . that was like falling off a cliff, but when you'd started, there was nothing else in the world like it: the heat of the lights and the music in your head and all around you, and the people you knew best in the world transformed. Sparko dancing so that you wished he'd never stop, and Coral singing, and giving you goosepimples because you'd never heard anything so perfect in your whole life. The sounds she'd made kept going round and round in Lydia's head.

"Can I come in?" It was Dweebsie.

"Yeah, OK." Lydia had wondered briefly where he'd got to and then just forgotten all about him. She felt bad about that. He was so sweet, and now here he was.

"I thought I'd wait until the rest of them had gone. I didn't want to say the same things everyone else was saying. And I didn't want to speak to anyone else. Just you."

Lydia smiled. "I'm glad you're here. I thought you'd gone home. It's your show, Dweebsie. You put all the words together for us to say. You must be so pleased. We couldn't have done it without you . . . so thank you."

Dweebsie hung his head in embarrassment. "It wasn't my show. It was yours . . . all of you, really, but especially you. You were . . . I haven't really got a proper word for what you were. I'll never forget tonight, that's what I wanted to say. Never."

Lydia sprang up and hugged him. "Are you coming to meet the others?"

"If you want me to."

"Of course I want you to, Dweebsie. Don't be silly."

"I didn't mean to bring this up tonight, but . . . Lydia, are you sure you still want to go out with me? You should say if you don't."

In the space of less than a second, all sorts of thoughts flashed through Lydia's mind. Sparko . . . he didn't love her . . . Coral . . . her friend now . . . how much easier life was when Dweebsie was there . . . and how he felt about her. Perhaps his feelings would be strong enough for both of them. And she liked him so much . . . how could she hurt him? Just before Christmas, too. She said: "Don't be silly, Dweebsie. Can you carry my case?"

Dweebsie smiled, and said: "To the ends of the earth."

"No, silly, just across the road to Lucia."

In honour of the occasion, Ettore had pushed all the tables together and put out plates of panettone for everyone. "On the house!" he said. "For such talented dancers and singers . . . it move my heart to see. Is thank you for my ticket."

"We're glad you liked it," said Pammy. "Come again tomorrow, if you like."

"I will come!" said Ettore. "I will bring my wife and my children. This is not something every day you see."

Sparko and Coral and Lydia and Dweebsie made their way through the quiet streets.

"Look," said Lydia, "it's snowing . . . "

"Amazing," said Sparko. "It almost never snows here."

"It's going to be a white Christmas," said Coral. "I feel it in my bones. And next year's going to be the best year yet. I'm going to do so many things . . ."

"You should make a resolution to do your own Science homework. That'd be a good way to start the millennium."

Goodnights took a long time when they got to Coral's house. Everyone had to hug and kiss everyone else.

" 'Night."

"See you tomorrow."

"See you."

"Sleep tight."

Then the girls shut the door behind them, and Sparko and Dweebsie made their way through the streets together, with the snow falling around them.

Sunday 8.00 p.m.
Walking home, I said, "I don't think he's that keen on her. What sort of kiss do you think it was? Was there actual lip contact? Or was it lip to cheek, or lip to corner of mouth?"

"I think it was lip to corner of mouth, but maybe it was lip to cheek?"

"It wasn't **full-frontal snogging** though, was it?"

"No."

"I think she went for full-frontal and he converted it into lip to corner of mouth . . ."

Saturday 6.58 p.m.
Lindsay was wearing a thong! I don't understand **thongs** – what is the point of them? They just go up your bum, as far as I can tell!

Wednesday 10.30 p.m.
Mrs Next Door complained that **Angus** has been frightening their poodle again. He stalks it. I explained, "Well, he's a Scottish wildcat, that's what they do. They stalk their prey. I have tried to train him but he ate his lead."

*"This is very funny – very, very funny. I wish I had read this when I was a teenager, it really is **very funny**."* Alan Davies

Also available from Piccadilly Press, by
JONATHAN MERES

When Mr, 'hey, call me Dave'
Sissons suggests that 5B keep
a diary for a whole year,
reactions are decidedly mixed!
Yo! Diary! grants us exclusive
access to all areas of six very
different fifteen-year-old
minds:

Seb – the rebel and
'Spokesdood for a
generation';
Meera – a girl obsessed
with astrology;
Steven Stevens – so good
his parents named him twice;
Clare – the local neighbourhood Eco Warrior;
Mandy – Ms Personality and Karaoke Queen, and
Craig – convinced that he's the only virgin on the entire
planet.

Jonathan Meres has written a riveting and hilarious tale of
teenagers teetering on the edge of the millennium! It's a
story of changes, drama, love, intrigue and plenty of good
old angst! And that's just in the first week!

*"Meres' strong, irreverent characterisation and sharp humour
(he was a stand-up comedian with his own radio show) make
this a book that will achieve an effortless following."*
Publishing News

Laetitia Alexandra Rebecca Fitt has more problems than just an odd name. Like three younger brothers (euk!), a baby sister, and an older sister with very strong views on life (Alex's). Having crazily busy parents may mean freedom – which is cool – but it also means they never notice Alex. Added to this, the love of Alex's life (Kevin in Year 12) doesn't know she exists. And then there's friends and parties . . .

By the author of the *Help!* series: *Help! My Family is Driving Me Crazy!*, *Help! My Social Life is a Mess!* and *Help! Let Me Out of Here!* and of the titles *Boywatching!*, *Girls are From Saturn Boys are From Jupiter* and *How to be Completely Cool*.

Who'd have thought that Chloë – cool, rich and so sophisticated – would have anything in common with Sinead, who longs for popularity?

And who'd have suspected the problems lurking beneath Jasmin's sparkling smile? And if we're talking about mysteries, then just who is Nick – the fit, supercool guy, but what is he hiding?

And what of Sanjay, who finds his computer so much more user-friendly than people? As five very different teenagers struggle to cope with their changing lives they fall into a friendship which surprises them all . . .

"*. . . five teenagers from very different backgrounds, the fun and drama of their lives is drawn with humour and sensitivity.*"
Pick of the Paperbacks – The Bookseller

Cassie Lang is nearly sixteen, and she's never been on a proper date!

All the magazines, papers, TV and films tell her that this is the best time of her life and she should be doing everything – drugs, alcohol, boyfriends and 'it'. Where has she gone wrong?

When Cassie gets her first boyfriend she knows exactly what to expect: she's seen it, read it and heard it all. She's got her life sorted. But somehow in reality things just don't happen as they should . . .

A sharp, hilarious account of the differences between real life and the glamorous life the media says we should be living!

By the author of *Enter the Boy-zone* and *Girl Power*:
". . . *an invaluable guide to teenage life . . . Packed with case studies and handy checklists, it's also a great read.*"
Virgin Net

If you would like more information about books available from Piccadilly Press and how to order them, please contact us at:

Piccadilly Press Ltd.
5 Castle Road
London
NW1 8PR

Tel: 020 7267 4492
Fax: 020 7267 4493